There are themes and language present within this book that some people may find upsetting.

Castle Drum Publishing

Printed in the United States of America
First Printing, 2022
Second Edition: 2024
ISBN: 979-8-9872153-0-2
Castle Drum Publishing
www.castledrumpublishing.org
This novel's story and characters are fictitious. Certain long-standing institutions, agencies, and public offices are mentioned, but the characters involved are wholly imaginary.

*Darkness at the Edge
of Time:*

DUALITY

Castle Drum Publishing

TO MY WIFE AMY;
MY LIFE CHANGED WHEN I FIRST SAW YOU
SMILE

Chapter One

...because doesn't every story start with chapter one?

"You have a little burn there on your neck, Jack," the young firefighter said as he sat down next to his commander on the hood of a rusted-out Chrysler K-car that proudly displayed a quarter panel and a door that were different colors than the rest of its body. The young man stared at his commander's injury for a few more seconds and realized he had undersold the wound. It was a significant burn and would need treatment. However, he decided not to correct his statement. His commander seemed distracted. A blank look had come over Jack. Just before the junior fireman was going to repeat himself, the response he was looking for finally came.

"Thanks, Jerzy. I can feel it. Starting to really sting. Is it blistering yet?" Jack began to reach up and feel it, but decided to keep his dirty hand away from the injury. Infection was the last thing he needed. Jack was well aware of how fast death could arrive, not just with fires and collapsed buildings, but with unseen microbes as well. That knowledge made him fight hypochondria every day.

"Yeah. It's starting to. Looks nasty," said Jerzy as he leaned in to see the wound better in the dim light and shadows of distant street lamps. "It won't get you a disability, but you're going to need to see the EMTs." He sat back and pulled out a pack of Camels. With a smooth dexterity, he tapped one out and fired it up. He held the pack out as he exhaled smoke in Jack's direction. Jerzy went through this ritual after every fire was extinguished.

"You know I quit a long time ago. Why do you always offer me one? Swear you're trying to kill me."

"I don't know. Misery loves company I guess...or maybe I'm the great tempter." Jerzy shook the pack in his face a little. Jack smiled and waved him off one more time.

"What I need is a temptress," sighed Jack with a weary voice.

This was a new declaration. It surprised Jerzy, who knew a few things about his commander's personal life, but only a few. Jack did not like to talk about himself. Jerzy hesitated at first, but as usual, decided to go with his gut instinct. "I hear that. Some little honey dressed up for Halloween...sexy little nurse outfit or a vampire or a French maid. Oh, oooh, one of those red vinyl and leather devil costumes," Jerzy rambled on with the excitement of the young and virile. Of all the men and one woman in Jack's engine company, he liked Jerzy the best. He was short in stature but long on fight. Jack had never seen him in a fistfight, but he had witnessed his strength and courage battling some nasty blazes. Yet, in the end, it was Jerzy's ability to make Jack break the stoic expression he usually held that won him over.

"You sound like you've really thought about this," said Jack with a laugh.

"Tomorrow's Halloween, Lieutenant. It'd be nice if it was on a weekend and not a

Wednesday, but we don't have a shift tomorrow, so it's a weekend to me. Course I went to

Halloween parties the last two weeks. You should've come."

"I wasn't up for that."

"Yeah...you know...I just thought...you know it's been a few years since...since Angie..."

The senior firefighter let the younger man be uncomfortable for a few more seconds. Then he let his comrade off the hook. "I appreciate it, Jerzy. I really do." Jack let it stand at that for a while, but he really did like Jerzy. He appreciated him trying to help, even if it was annoying at times. So, Jack decided to tell him more. "You see, Jordan," he started to say. The younger firefighter was a little startled, and not just because he used his real name. He had thought the conversation was over. "It's like when you've tasted the sweetest, most delicious peach in the world. Then someone offers you a nectarine. That nectarine may be just fine. It may be the best nectarine in the world, but it won't ever be as good as that peach. Things won't ever be that sweet again."

Jerzy did not like how serious the conversation had turned. "I get what you're saying,

Lieutenant." He paused and then added, "Well, maybe. I've never had a nectarine before."

"Seriously?" Jack choked back laughter.

"Yeah. My family wasn't big on fruit unless it was in a pie at McDonald's." A perplexed look came over Jack as he listened to Jerzy explain. "My mother liked to spoil us with sweets. What can I say? We didn't eat real healthy in the Carrera household." Jack just raised his eyebrows and shook his head.

"You do know it's something that looks like a peach, except it doesn't have the fuzzy..."

"Yeah, Jack. I know. I know. Make fun of the guy from the city, who never saw a cow till he was twenty-one."

"You never saw a cow till you were twenty-one?" asked Jack in his most surprised voice. They both chuckled hard for a few moments before allowing a relative silence to fall.

"No. I'm not kidding," confirmed Jerzy with emphasis.

Jack was enjoying the break from the stress of their jobs and hoped he could keep it alive with a little more teasing. "No wonder with a name like Jerzy." He let that hang in the air for a moment but got no response from his colleague. "Hey, I've been meaning to ask. How'd you get the name, Jerzy anyways? You said you grew up in Pittsburgh."

"Well, that was only partially true. I came here in '89 when I was thirteen. It was a fresh start for my mom and me. I'm originally from Camden, across the river from Philadelphia."

"I see. So, people at your new school started calling you Jerzy."

"Not exactly. I never liked my name all that much. Didn't like that it was a name for girls too. Around that time I was listening to a lot of Public Enemy and NWA. I thought I was going to be the first big, Hispanic rapper. Straight outta Mexico, you know? I was going to be the Latino Chuck D. So, I told everyone my name was Jerzy. It actually worked pretty well for me. Everyone thought I had all this street cred. My mom got us into a nice school district…well, I mean relatively speaking. It wasn't exactly North Allegheny or Fox Chapel. Still, I was going to school with a bunch of white kids with names that ended in 'ski and 'vich, you know, people that used to work in the steel mills." Jerzy laughed long and hard. Jack did not see what was so humorous.

He smiled and said, "What's so funny about steel mills. They always looked like a job in hell to me."

"Hah! That's saying something, seeing what we do for a living. No. That's not it. I was thinking back to a buddy of mine's grandmother. So Mike, my buddy, told his grandma my name was Jerzy. He was trying to tease me about my chosen rap name and was emphasizing the spelling to his grandma. She suddenly tells me that my name is Polish and she starts to correct me on how I pronounce it."

"How do you pronounce it?" asked Jack.

"I don't remember, but that's not the funny part."

"No?"

"Nah. Here's what's funny." Jerzy giggled a little, which made Jack's brow furrow. "She tells me that my real name and Jerzy mean the same thing. They're just different forms of George. How's that for a slap in the face. My supposed-to-be- cool rap name turns out to be the same name I can't stand. Guess you can't escape who you are, destiny and all that." Jerzy thought about that for a microsecond and decided that once again, he did not like the way the conversation was going. He took a drag on his cigarette and said, "Destiny; that was the name of this hot girl at the last party I went to. Now she was a fire that I did not want to escape from. I'm telling you, you should come with me sometime, boss."

"I thought I told you I was too old to play dress-up."

"Never too old if the women keep you young." "Is that your mantra?" asked Jack.

"I don't know what mantra means, but I like the sound of it, so I'm going to say, yes."

"And you think there was a lovely lady there for this old carcass?" Jack pointed at himself and raised an eyebrow in disbelief. He liked acting as if he was the father figure, even though he was only in his mid-thirties. It gave him a little bit of distance from the people under his command.

"No thinking about it. I know it. There was this one chica there, and she was dressed in some school girl's outfit. She actually wanted to talk about the school and how authentic her outfit was. Never heard of the school, some crazy name like Hog Farts or somethin'. Anyway, she was young enough to be tight but old enough to know how to use it. You know what I mean?"

Jack was staring at the two charred homes intently, trying to listen to Jerzy, but distracted by something, something he could not pinpoint. Was it a sound? A flicker of light? A smell? He turned to his subordinate and absent-mindedly said, "Yeah. I know what you mean."

"Had this whole sexy librarian vibe goin' on with those glasses." Jack was no longer paying even polite attention to Jerzy's banter. His senses were heightened. Hairs were standing up. His eyes darted over the two smoldering ruins. Even his burned neck seemed to be stinging more. The pain just made him more agitated and intense. "...and that little kilt she had..."

"Is the FM here yet?" Jack interrupted.

"Fire Marshall? No. Why? You see something suspicious?" He did not let Jack answer.

"Better not be arson, man. We don't need no damn Devil's Night here in Pittsburgh."

Jack's head snapped around to face Jerzy again. "What did you say?" It was forceful enough that Jerzy jumped a little and dropped his still burning cigarette. There was little left, so he did not bend over to pick up the butt. He could see the intense interest in his commander's eyes and was instead completely focused on him.

"What? Devil's Night. You've heard of it. Out in Detroit. October thirtieth. Every year the idiots try to burn their city down. From what I've heard, they got it under control now, some movement called Angel's Night or some..."

"What makes you think it's Devil's Night here?"

Jerzy was growing uncomfortable again, but for a different reason. He had never seen his commander's eyes so intense. "Easy, Jack. Relax. It's just we've had more calls tonight on the radio than we usually get, just a coincidence. The Burgh was once the city of red hot steel and fire, hell with the lid torn off they called it, but no more. No, sir. No Devil's Night, no worries, Lieutenant. Right?"

"If something's not right, we need to get ahead of the curve, or it will take us down."

Jack's response did nothing to calm Jerzy's anxiety. Why was his commander so upset, so extreme? He tried to settle him down, feeling as though it was his comments that had agitated his commander. "Just me reaching for things, Jack. Sorry. You know how people

love the drama. We all look for big events to worry about, especially so soon after 9-11. Like that Y2K crap last year. Remember that? Turned out to be nothing. Seems like there's always some big threat. Always got to be something we're afraid of. No Devil's Night in Pittsburgh. No, sir."

"Still, I want to see the FM when he gets..."

"Here comes Oakland's chief." Interjected Jerzy. "We can ask him."

The PBF battalion chief, normally a charismatic leader, stared straight ahead as he approached from the right. Without breaking stride, he turned and gazed into Jack's eyes.

"Lieutenant Lear, she wanted me to tell you that the undercroft is ready. Time grows short." He turned his head away from them and methodically continued walking up the street. As he walked away, he said in a soft, almost feminine voice, "Jack, you know the child, Elizabeth, must never ascend the throne." Jack's brow became furrowed. Jerzy's lip curled and his eyes squinted. A perplexed look came over both their faces.

"What the hell was that all..." Jerzy began to ask.

It only took an instant for the growing darkness to be ripped apart, torn along jagged lines of light and heat. The black stillness to their right, beyond the perimeter of their floodlights, lit up. The radiant brilliance of an explosion reflected back from the houses across the street faster than any human's eyes could tell. Jack, Jerzy, and all the other firefighters who had begun cleaning up, felt the shock wave of expanding gases rock the ground. The impact of compressed air knocked the two of them off the abandoned car. Their eyes and ears became useless for a short span as the sound deafened the firefighters, and the ball of flame roaring out of the row home's lower floor blinded them for a moment. The next house on the street was now filled with fire. The expanding flames made their pupils squeeze shut. The heat briefly felt like a thousand bees stinging their faces. Glass, wood, metal, and brick shrapnel peppered the street for a couple of seconds and then was gone from the air around them.

Gravity had recalled all of it once more. Thankfully, no large pieces had hit them.

Jack was the first one up. He looked at the house, now totally engulfed in flames, and shouted, "Damn it to hell!" Then something on the sidewalk caught his attention, and for a moment, the newly born fire was forgotten. One of his firefighters was laid out on the crumbling cement. Jerzy was now up as well, and they both began to move. They arrived at the side of Elaine Sachs simultaneously. She was lying on her back, appearing lifeless. Her helmet was in the street. Blood was pouring from a nasty cut and contusion on the side of her head. It was near the temple, which increased Jack's worry even more. He began checking her vital signs. "Got a pulse. Respiratory's not visible." Her chest was not noticeably rising and falling. Nor could Jack feel any breath from her mouth and nose. Nothing rattled Jack more than seeing one of his firefighters injured. The word amongst his superiors was that he did not have the ability to be calm in a fight. They felt a detachment allowed for cool decisions when under stress. Jack thought their analysis was a load of crap, but he also knew he had been passed over twice for brigade command. None of that mattered now. Before deciding to start rescue breathing on Elaine, he screamed at Jerzy, "I thought you said that house was clear!" At that, Elaine began to cough. Jerzy helped turn her onto her side. She moaned, but still did not open her eyes.

"It is. I mean it was," answered Jerzy. He looked away from Jack and Elaine toward the house. "Me and Tommy checked it top to bottom."

Jack did not even acknowledge his plea. "Get some pressure on that wound," he ordered dismissively. Jerzy did as he was told. He pulled out his undershirt, tore off a section from the bottom of it, and balled it up. Jerzy slid his leg under Elaine's head to give her support. She was moving, but still seemed groggy and had not spoken. He gently applied pressure. Jack was still fighting through the fog of confusion that comes from an unexpected explosion one door down. His eyes squinted for a moment, trying to make sense of what was happening around him. For a moment he focused on Jerzy being so caring and compassionate with Elaine. Jack saw more than one comrade helping another. Jerzy had the distressed look of someone whose friend is in terrible danger. Usually Jerzy was insulting Elaine, calling her a variety of synonyms for lesbian. Perhaps, it was a classic act to divert attention from the fact that he actually had feelings for her. Jack shook that thought off. There was no time for that sort of gossipy speculation. No other wounds appeared as Jack checked her body thoroughly for blood, burns, and bruises. Suddenly, he stood up, ramrod straight. "You hear that?"

"What?" responded Jerzy, more out of confusion than curiosity. Jack could tell from the response that his colleague did not hear it. There it was again. It was low, but the frequency was unmistakable. No human can ignore that pitch of sound. It brings out our most nurturing side, but it will drive a person insane if exposed to it for too long.

Jack looked down at his subordinate and yelled, "Damn it, Jordan. How could you miss that? What the hell were you and Tom doing?"

"What are you..." Jack had no more time for answering Jerzy's questions.

"Keep treating Elaine till the EMTs get here. I gotta go in."

"Wait! Jack! No!" It was too late. Jack was gone. The house was becoming an inferno, and he had to get in and out as fast as possible. The bottom floor, which had blown out, was roaring. Jack could see the combustion on the lower floor was beginning to consume the upper. For the briefest of moments, he thought about getting his helmet and SCBA. Even his coat would be nice, but there was no time. The old row house was a tinderbox, and he knew from experience it would soon be engulfed in flames.

He bounded up onto the porch in two steps and burst through the front doorway. The blast had been kind enough to knock the door off its hinges. For several seconds he stood in the entranceway, unsure what to do. His emotions swirled around in his head. There was a mixture of fear and fascination with the fire. It was growing, crawling up the walls, always consuming. Yet, the driving instinct was to find the baby he had heard from the street. Only now, all he could hear was the fire. The idea that the cry had been imagined began to take root in his brain. Was it just the ringing in his head from the blast? Then the piercing sound of another cry hit his ears. Up the stairs he climbed with a speed born out of desperation. The first door was closed. He felt the cheap wood. It was relatively cool, which he expected. The fire had not yet had time to dry, ignite, and consume the second floor, but it was coming. It was growing.

Jack opened the door and went in. There was some smoke, but not enough to asphyxiate or even cloud his vision. He quickly ascertained that there was nothing to be found there. Back in the hallway, Jack peered toward the far end. There were three more rooms off the hallway and what looked to be a bathroom at the end. The door to his left was also closed. Reflexively, from his training, he checked it again. It was also cool enough to not expect a blast when he opened it. His hand reached for the knob and frustration grew from his fingers up to his heart. It was locked. Another cry hit his ears and he knew what must be done. Jack wished he had an ax or bar to pry it open, but he was a big man, and despite the house being from an older period of time, when quality supposedly mattered, the door did not look that strong. He backed up, surged forward, and placed his boot right below the doorknob. It did not crash open, but Jack felt the bolt give. Once more he kicked, shattering the wood around the door's lock.

It swung open. There was a moment of peace, and then just like opening the door of an oven, a blast of heat hit him in the face. It knocked him back on his heels, but he did not go down. The fire had already reached this room. After the initial wave of energy passed, he cautiously went in, expecting the baby to be trapped in a crib. Yet, there was no crib, no play-pen. There was nothing, no furniture at all. Jack was amazed at the amount of fire though. The room was becoming enveloped in dark crimson flames. Their color and intensity captured Jack's attention. The smoke was rolling too and that made Jack snap out of his momentary trance. He realized he had to do a quick search.

Kneeling to get under the smoke, Jack began to sweep the floor with his eyes. What he saw instantly became burned into his consciousness. To his right, a fine pair of black, leather shoes walked out of the smoke and flames. Jack's eyes rose as he did. When he reached his full height he was face to face with a vision that seemed so incongruent it stunned Jack into silence and paralysis for a moment. Jack was the stereotypical firefighter. He was as straight as an arrow, but this had to be the most beautiful man he had ever seen. His face was completely out of place with the destruction swirling around him. Their hair was a rich blonde and perfectly cut. There was not one strand out of place despite the whirling air generated by the fire's perpetual hunger for oxygen. Clean-shaven, Jack could see the sharp outlines of his cheekbones, which seemed to form perfect question marks complete with dimples. A nose that was not too thick and not too thin led down to full lips and a strong chin. Yet, it was the man's eyes that captured and kept Jack's gaze. His face, particularly with the curl of his lips and those dimples, seemed friendly. The eyes were not. They seemed to be carved from anthracite, and the flames' reflection danced over them.

He took a few more steps and was face to face with Jack, but did not speak. It seemed he wanted Jack to get the full measure of him. And he did. The man was tall, several inches larger than Jack, who stood six foot two. He seemed lean, but not thin. The dark, bespoke suit he wore showed his physique with exquisite perfection. It hung as if draped on a mannequin.

In fact, the only thing that seemed out of place on the man was a small bundle in his left arm. Jack quickly realized that the bundle was a baby wrapped in a blanket. It looked like a baby burrito. As if to confirm this, the child began to cry. It was just what Jack needed to bring him back to the reality that they were standing in the middle of a house that was clearly going to burn to the foundation. Collapse was inevitable and coming soon, but Jack could still not initiate action. The man's appearance was simply too enigmatic and entrancing to be ignored. The man had walked right off the cover of a magazine. Yet, the black eyes seemed like sunspots on the surface of a star. There was something wrong here. It was all wrong. He watched the stranger run a smooth hand over the baby's head and then trace a manicured finger down the child's nose. He tapped him on the nose gently and then touched the baby's lips. A lovely "Shhhh," was somehow heard over the terrible noise of wood being consumed.

The infant stopped crying. Jack's mouth hung open in a stupor.

There was a soft aura around the man. This eerie glow, Jack quickly recognized, did not emanate from the flames growing larger around him. The firefighter had never seen anything like it. Still, Jack was a more pragmatic than curious man. There were more important things to do. Wondering whether the man appeared to have some angelic halo or not could wait. Even though it did not seem to be bothering the man in the sharp suit, the heat and smoke were having an impact on Jack. He had begun to cough as his lungs reflexively tried to force the ash and other impurities from his body. His skin was drying. Cells were dying. Fluid was flowing, and blisters were bubbling.

"C'mon Mister. We gotta go. The whole place is going up!" he shouted at the stranger.

"I think we have some time to talk, Jack." The fireman was dumbfounded, not simply because the stranger knew his name, but due to the observation that the man's lips barely moved. It looked as if he had whispered the sentence. Yet, Jack heard it clearly above the din of the fire, as if when the man spoke the crack and roar of the blaze became muted.

"Who...umm." Jack swallowed a cough, but could not hold it down. His mouth was too dry. It built up and then burst out in a spasmodic rasp. Finally, Jack was able to ask, "Who are you?"

"My name is Malachi Morgenstern." As the sound of his voice died away the whoosh and screams of the fire sucking up oxygen returned.

"Well, Mr. Stern, you..." There was more coughing. "You and your kid must leave. Now!" Jack tried to use his voice to reassert his authority. It did not work.

The man smiled softly, revealing perfect, white teeth, and said "This pathetic wretch is not mine." The words were harsh, yet it sounded like a song in his voice. He lifted the swaddled babe up with one hand as if offering it as proof of paternity. "May I introduce you to one Dionysus Ankou. He is sixty-one days old. Father is a Creole, who went back to New Orleans sixty days ago. His mother is a dancer-slash-prostitute here in Pittsburgh." Morgenstern's voice was anchorman smooth, sounding like he was introducing a game show contestant. "Her hobbies include smoking crystal meth and...well, that about sums it up."

"That's a tragic story, but we got..."

"Wait," whispered Morgenstern. And Jack did. "It does not end there." He lowered the baby and raised his other hand to emphasize the importance of what he was about to say. "I have not explained the best part of the story. His mother is working the pole tonight. However, she was a responsible mother and got a babysitter." His mellifluous speech was truly entrancing, but Jack could not help but watch the flames reaching the tops of the walls as he spoke. The smoke curled in toward the center of the room, but then seemed to pour from the ceiling to the floor before reaching them. "Of course, the tweaker she left him with is passed out in the next room."

A thunderous crash erupted behind the dark man, who never moved, not the slightest flinch. Jack jumped back a half step as the far wall collapsed, creating a shower of flames, debris, and embers. Jack was incredulous. Two things were revealed to him. They made him stand in awe for several seconds. There was a man on the floor in the next room. That, however, was not the amazing part. It was the fire circling him that began to scare Jack in a new way. The flames were not just burning in a circle around him. They were literally circling the man on the floor as though they had truly come to life. If that had been all, he could have kept his nerves calm, but instead, his fear intensified as a huge, sinister looking, black dog, with a shaggy mane, calmly walked through the new opening in the wall. He sauntered up to the side of Morgenstern. The beast bared his teeth at Jack and then barked. The sound hit the firefighter's chest like the shock wave of a small explosive. It made his heart skip a beat, as the right ventricle went out of time. He stammered, "What is that?"

"That is my dear companion, Cù-Sith. He has barked once, which means that time has begun to run out. Death is coming."

"Then let's get the hell out of here!" Jack took a step toward the door even though his mind was telling him to go get the man in the other room.

"I will not be coming with you."

"I can't carry the baby and that man," yelled Jack.

"True. For a meth addict, you would think he would weigh less." The man smiled at his own witticism. Jack could not decide if he was friendly or a complete sociopath. "You have a choice, Jack. Who lives? Who dies? Ohhh the power." He let the last statement hang in the heated air then added, "But what a terrible responsibility it is."

"Look! I am ordering you to take that baby out of here. You can still..."

With a calmness that was unsettling and aggravating, the man interrupted the lieutenant. "With all due respect, Jack, I do not take orders from anyone." The man's intransigence was being directly converted into the firefighter's anger. That was when things went from bad to worse.

"Jack! Jack, where are you? Lieutenant Lear! This house is coming down!"

"No. No. Damn it. No!" Jack turned toward the door and screamed, "Jerzy get out of here!" Another shock wave exploded from the dog's lungs. It seemed like a hammer blow to the fireman's chest. Though barely audible over the fire, another yell from down the stairs answered it. Which one was more horrifying was debatable.

"I can't get to you, Jack. The stairs are cut off." The fireman's gaze was now locked on the stranger's coal-black eyes. In a few seconds, Jack had become certain that the man was not a normal human being. He was a total psycho. Chaos shone in his black eyes. He wanted them all to die, and now Jack's colleague and friend was in danger as well. "Jack! Can you hear me, Jack?

"Twice now Cù-Sith has spoken," warned Morgenstern in his smooth, yet ominous voice. "The third time will be the end. Someone must die."

For the first time since his wife had passed away, Jack felt like crying. However, this was not due to grief. His emotions were being torn in too many directions. His anger wanted him to tear into this pretty boy. His fear wanted him to run. His loyalty told him to save his friend. An emptiness that came from the dark void in his heart asked him to just lie down and let the flames finally win. Yet, his compassion and love won out. He would save them all, and this crazy fool and his dog would not stop him. "Give me the kid," he demanded. We're goin' out the window. Then I'll be back for the methhead."

"Sorry, Jack. I told you. Death is coming. The gas is about to explode."

"Jack!" hollered Jerzy from downstairs once more as he put an ax blade into the collapsed burning banister, trying to clear a path for a rescue attempt. Jack ignored his yell.

"Well now, the trick's on you, Morgan. We had all the gas lines shut down."

"Good planning on your part," agreed the beautiful shadow. "Yet, a meth lab really tries to avoid paper trails. They have a large propane tank in the back. The initial explosion from their chemicals did not rupture it, but with this much heat, the pressure is building. And I can tell that Cù-Sith is about to bark again. Who will it be, Jack? The wee baby? Your friend downstairs? Or the poor man behind me, who as we speak has a mother, one Edie Faulk, desperately searching for him, trying to save him from the damnation of drug addiction." The man took a step back. "She knows he could be something great." Another few steps were taken into the now enveloping flames. His right hand swept toward the prone man. "All he really wants is to marry the baby's mother, Venus. He's known her for years, and he honestly wants to be a father to little Dionysus." Smoke was now filling the room, but Jack thought he saw the circle of fire stop and reverse direction. It was running counter-clockwise now. "If only he could just get clean." Morgenstern seemed to be fading out as smoke began to roll in front of him. "He could save them. Save them all."

"Give me that baby," demanded Jack.

"Of course." And with that, he threw the child into the air and disappeared into the next room, where the fire still circled the addict like a phantasm.

"What is wrong..." Jack could not finish the question. His legs were already moving. Perhaps it was his life-saving training that made him react, but most likely it was simply his humanity. The rescue worker bolted forward and in a move he had not done since playing centerfield for his high school baseball team, Jack slid under the falling baby and made a basket catch. The instant the young one hit his hands the boy began to cry. It was a good thing. The infant had been so silent while Morgenstern was taunting Jack that he thought the man may have already killed the child. Jack's happiness, however, did not last, not even for a full second.

In a flash of fire and recognition, he saw that his legs had slid into the inferno. Something flammable must have spilled or fallen on him because his legs were now burning. He twisted his upper body away from the fire and pushed the baby toward the one area of the floor that was not in flames. Jack rolled back and forth then began pounding on his pants with his bare hands, knowing they were being burned but having too much adrenaline flowing to feel it. He stood up and looked to the other room. The psychopathic runway model was gone. Yet, the addict remained. The crazy man was right. A terrible choice had to be made, yet, in the end, it turned out to be an easy one. He scooped up the baby and took one look at the doorway. It was engulfed in flames. There was no exit there. He went to the window at the front of the room, facing the street. The row home was an old house with framed windows that you had to slide up to open. With everything he had, Jack tried to lift the window. Not one millimeter did it raise. "You have got to be..." He saw the heads of the nails that held the panes of glass and wood frames in place. The glass reflected the dance of all the flames around him as if mocking his predicament. There was no time for yelling and screaming in frustration. Jack moved back from the window, got as much of his hands over the baby's head as he could, and yelled, "Get outta here, Jerzy! Get the hell out of here!"

Then he heard a distant bark that he would always recognize, always remember. It made him turn toward the addict's room one last time. The room and the prone man were gone, swept away by a wall of smoke and flame. Jack did not allow himself to think about the horror of dying from asphyxiation, either from the smoke or from the effects of superheated air. Worse still would be to die from the shock of your body being torched. A lightning bolt of fear ripped through his entire spine and into his brain. He looked to his right and saw the lights of the trucks outside dancing off the plate glass window. Jack backed up a few more feet and felt the fire reach his back. The skin began to bubble up and sizzle as his shirt ignited. His legs exploded with the energy of total despair as he surged toward the window. On his second step, he heard a weakened voice from behind him pleading in a guttural scream, "Help me! Help me!" His foot hit a third time and he heard another voice mixed with the desperate plea.

"Jack! Where are you?"

He launched his body forward. What athleticism he still had left came rushing back into his muscles. In mid-air, he twisted his body so that his head and shoulder would hit the glass first. It also shielded the child from the collision. The old window shattered into myriad pieces. An instant later Jack hit the shingles of the overhang that covered the porch, driving some of those pieces into the flesh of his arms, but none hit the baby. His body rolled onto his back and then became airborne. Falling, he heard the explosion rip through the house and saw the flames briefly erupt from any available opening. His world went black before he hit the ground, but he did not lose consciousness. He lost his breath and the baby. No air seemed to be going into his lungs, but he could hear the little one somewhere to his left, wailing like a banshee. Jack knew the child would be all right. The infant had landed on top of him. Scared was all he was. If he had not been blinded, he would have felt more concern. Burning pieces of the house fell all around them, but miraculously none hit the child. The row house became one large conflagration. The burned-out home to its one side reignited. The untouched home on its other side began to burn. The entire neighborhood was in peril, but Jack could not see or hear that. All he heard was the muffled crying of a two-month-old boy. Yet, all his mind could focus on was a friend that had been left behind.

"Jerzy!" Jack tried to scream, but nothing came out. His lungs were still not working. However, the pain receptors in his body seemed to work all too well. Instinctively, Jack knew that he had, at the minimum, broken multiple ribs. The intense agony in his head and the lack of vision made him think he also had a concussion. That did not worry him. It was the pain in his upper back and the absence of it in his lower body that brought a new wave of fear. The adrenaline and stinging hurt overloaded his mind. Jack began slipping into shock. The last conscious thought he had was the first words he was able to speak. "Jordan....Jer...get out..." It all faded to black.

Chapter Seventeen

...because every story should start at the beginning.

At just sixteen, Jack was still a boy, but for the standards of his time, he was a man. His father and mother had explained to him that, sadly, they could offer him nothing as their first-born, but perhaps his uncle, could provide some work. After all, his uncle owned a large farm with a great number of livestock. A further inducement was the fact that he had four sisters, all much younger, all with hungry mouths to feed. Not even the oldest one would be ready to get married for several more years. His parents made sure that he understood the situation. He felt love for his parents, the kind you feel from the innate connection you share, but there was no warmth. He had always questioned them, even after his father would lose his temper and beat him, or his mother would run out of patience and berate him. Despite all his best intentions, he could not stop challenging them. It felt downright sinful, but he could not help but feel they were, to put it politely, not as smart as he was. They were simple folk and had accepted their place in the world. Jack could not.

He had a few mates, but they also seemed content with their lot in life. It was obvious to Jack that his friends were simple folk as well. They had to be.

Why else would they consent to this miserable life they lived, paying exorbitant rent, basically outright extortion? They scraped by with barely enough food and heat to survive each winter. Why should they stay? Why should they agree to live this wretched life? Jack told his friends what his mother believed; the Second Coming would arrive in just thirteen months. The year 1500 AD would be the end. The signs were all there she told Jack, and he told his friends. All of them found it funny. Jack's mother was a strange one. That they could all agree on. But they laughed at Jack just as hard when he suggested they strike out on their own and break away from the tedium of their existence. None of them could imagine the world beyond. They were not the only ones to laugh at him.

The Sabbat of Sisters, which is what he called the little witches, much to his mother's chagrin and offense, was no comfort to him either. Their minds were more limited than his friend's. They were cowed by their father's volcanic temper and reduced to tears by their mother's use of guilt, or the threat of removing her love. It did not make them little angels, as his mother called them on her good days. It just made them cowards who hid in their meanness to each other. It was the only thing they were good at. When he would try to talk to them about the larger world and all of his dreams, their only response was to giggle. So, when his mother gave him a letter of introduction to his uncle and his father wished him Godspeed, it was a blessing, not the painful separation it would have been for most.

Fortune had been with him. His uncle, bereft of children himself, had been more than happy to welcome Jack to his minor estate. However, that welcome did not become a miraculous turn of events. There was no sudden adoption. His uncle did not immediately change his final will and testament. What he did do was give his nephew a job and a place to live. That place was in his barn. Occasionally, his uncle and aunt might invite him inside their manor home to dine with them. Usually, it was just hard work from before sunrise to sundown, except Sundays, which served as a temporary respite. There were only a few menial tasks to do on that day. His uncle did not force him to attend services, and Jack was not strong in the faith, so he could relax by himself. Jack was not really part of his uncle's household, so the church did not punish him for Jack's unwillingness to darken the church door.

During those early days at his uncle's farm, he found himself pondering the direction his life should take. It took on even more meaning when his mother's apocalyptic predictions proved false. He had never taken his mother's ranting seriously, but he discovered something very strange when the year 1501 began. There was a touch of sadness in his heart. He certainly did not want the end of the world to happen, but he had hoped for something meaningful to come about. Secretly, he wanted his mother to have something she could be proud of, even if it was an apocalyptic prediction. It was an immature emotion he told himself, knowing his mother was crazy, yet yearning for her to be right, even if it was the end of days she was right about. Jack never saw his parents or sisters after the present year dawned. More and more he listened to and observed his uncle. Jack knew how to achieve the same good life his uncle had wrought, and he now understood the path that his life should follow.

Unbeknownst to Jack, the literal path he was on at this very moment was a most serendipitous one. In the preceding months, he had quickly moved from doing all the menial tasks that needed to be done on the farm to becoming his uncle's cowherd. Thirty-one head of White Park cattle walked the path with him. They were his uncle's pride and joy. Many people considered the cattle to be noble, even majestic. With their long horns and white hides, some went as far as to call them beautiful. Jack's uncle was one of them. Yet, as the young man broke over the rise from the stream that ran through the farm, he playfully jumped up on the stone fence that enclosed one of the pastures used for grazing and saw something truly elegant and alluring. With the additional three feet of height, it was easy for him to survey the surrounding area. It was at this moment that he saw a sight that made the magnificence of any animal quickly fade away. Before him was a figure of astonishing beauty.

The cattle kept plodding along, neither knowing that something momentous had happened, nor caring. They walked past Jack, but he was frozen in his tracks, a statue on top of a plinth of fieldstone. In the distance, a young maiden frolicked through the meadow he was passing by to get the bovines to the grazing pasture they were scheduled to use. She was about two hundred feet away from him and seemed to be chasing a butterfly. It was so innocent that it made Jack smile. However, not all of his thoughts were pure of heart. Even with her loose, poorly fitting smock, Jack could see that she was no child. She was a young woman with a lovely form. In a single heartbeat, Jack experienced a lightness in his chest that he could not recall ever feeling. The beats were speeding up and his face was flush. The young man did not know what love was, but this must be at least a fraction of it.

She took no notice of him, being purely focused on the random angles chosen by the butterfly with royal blue wings. The flowers, blooming fully in the June sunshine, seemed to dance around her as she passed through the meadow. Her blonde hair bounced and waved with every jaunty step. Jack swallowed hard. She was skipping away from him. The Holly Blue butterfly had decided to dart in the exact opposite direction from his position. He was seventeen and felt like he was on the verge of old- age if this girl scampered away from him. For the first time in his life, he knew what he wanted without any of the debate that usually raged in his mind, and it was about to be lost. If she took a few more steps he knew he would allow himself to fall into resignation as though the world had conspired against him...again. Without thinking he bellowed, "Hello!" The girl did not stop. Perhaps, it had only been loud in his mind. "Hello there!" he tried again.

The maiden took two more steps but slowed and on the third step came to a stop. As nonchalantly as possible she turned and spied the source of distraction. A most pleasant smile came over her face. Her arm rose up and with her hand she waved back and forth twice. And that was it. She turned away again, looking for her butterfly. "Hey!" he shouted. "Don't go." He leapt down from the fence. She stopped walking away as if waiting for him, but she did not turn back around. He pulled up beside her, slightly panting from his sprint across the meadow. A deep breath was taken in the attempt to conceal his desperation.

Before he could move in front of her, she turned, and asked, "Are you the Lord's son?" It set him back on his heels. He had not thought of an introduction as he ran across the field, but if he had, it would have been useless after that query.

"What? I don't..." And then it dawned on him what she meant. Tension momentarily left him as he realized he would not need to ask for clarification. "Ohh. No. No. I am the Master's nephew. I've just come here to work for him. So far, I have been mostly a cowherd."

"They look like magnificent creatures. Do you know they have royal bloodlines?"

"Some say they have been on these isles since the dawn of man." She giggled.

"Do you believe that? How could anyone know that? Seems so silly." He loved her laugh. It settled into a smile that transfixed him.

"Well...I..." He had no idea where to go with the conversation. It made him nervous, but that was all right. It was anxiety that told him he wanted to do well. "My name's Jack. May I ask what your name is?"

"Of course, you may ask, but I may not tell." She smiled again. It seemed to be a natural state for her, along with bright eyes and a nimbleness about her movements. "That is, unless you tell me your story. Is it an amazing story?"

"Well, umm, I don't really know...I mean I don't think so." She made a faux frown.

"How about your name then?"

"My name? But, I said...my name is Jack."

"Maybe you are just a smidge daft," teased the maiden.

"What?"

She giggled again. "I meant your last name, Jack."

"I don't...I mean...I'm just Jack."

Her smile faded for a moment. She shook her head a few times with a false air of exasperation. "What's your family name?"

"I don't know," said Jack with an honesty born of true ignorance.

"Hasn't anyone ever called you anything but Jack?" she asked with a tilt of her head.

A look of perplexity now came over him. "Jack, son of Daniel. That's about it."

"Danielson? No, that's no good," she declared. "Now I have to find the answer to my question before I go."

Jack was confused by the statement but focused instead on its last word. "Don't go. I mean, I would like to talk to you."

"Wanting gets us up in the morning." Her smile was radiant.

"I'm not sure I…"

"What was your mother's last name?" she queried with mock seriousness.

"I don't know that she had one."

"You, Jack, are a riddle. You said the Master of the home there beyond these fields is your uncle?"

"Yes."

The interrogation continued. "On your mother's side or your father's?"

"He's my mother's brother."

"Well, what is his name?" She pushed him toward the end.

"Edward Landseer."

"Landseer. That's it. That's your mother's name as well."

"Right. That makes sense." Jack really did not understand, but he was not about to tell her that. He wanted this moment to go on as long as possible.

"But, I don't think that fits you. Seems too harsh. Maybe something a little different. I know." This time she did not giggle but burst out in a hardy laugh. "It's similar, but not so serious. And it was right in front of me the whole time." Jack just stared at her quizzically.

"Someday you can have my name."

"What?" He was confused as all kinds of thoughts rushed into his head.

"I think it fits you."

"Well, how..."

"That was a good story right there. See, now you can have a story about how you got your name." Her eyes lit up like the sun and her cheeks, lips, and teeth beamed in their reflection.

"But you never told me what yours was." Her smile now became slightly mischievous. He had never seen a smile like hers. Every man or woman in his family seemed to have a stern expression permanently etched on their face. She seemed fresh as a flower. In addition to her eyes, she had beautiful teeth, straight and a shade of white he had only seen in a toddler's laugh.

"No. No, I did not." She started walking away from him. "Your royal and ancient cows are getting away from you, Jack." He turned and saw that she was right. They were not in much danger of escaping, but he certainly did not want to take a chance. Nor did he want his uncle or one of the other laborers to see him standing in a field of flowers talking to a girl while the animals meandered.

"Will I ever get to see you again?"

"Of course you will, you silly man." "When?"

"You'll see me in your dreams." She laughed as she turned away and began to skip through the field of flowers. Jack knew that was the end of the moment. He already knew in his heart that it would become a cherished memory. Some things are so amazing that you know it right away. It doesn't require any reflection.

Chapter Two

...because the end is the beginning is the end.

Jack opened his eyes, but the image was so out of place that all he could do was shake his head a few times and blink. In the palm of his right hand was a small device about the size of a graham cracker. It looked like a mirrored piece of glass from a picture frame, but it was only about the thickness of a credit card. It did not have any buttons, wires, or antennas. Jack sensed that it was something more than a piece of glass, some type of technology. That was not all he sensed. He looked away from the device for a moment and saw the wheels on his chair. Tears began to build up in his eyes and almost immediately overflowed down his cheeks. Just beyond his hands were his withered legs. Jack scanned them momentarily, but felt nothing physically or emotionally. There were too many things hitting his mind at one time to make sense of it all. His hands were functional but clearly scarred. They had been burned a long, long time ago. Finally, his attention came back to the electronic tool he held. Perhaps it was self-preservation, but his mind told him the device was more interesting than his atrophied legs or burned hands. One side of it was entirely transparent. The other side was black. It was so thin Jack could not even see how it was held together. He turned it over once and when the glass side came up again there was a picture of a lovely, young woman staring at him. Without even a conscious thought he said, "What the...what is this?" He was not sure if he was talking about what he held in his hand or the wheelchair or the entire situation, but it was the electronic device that responded.

"Good morning, Jack." It was a friendly voice, but the woman did not seem quite real. She was very attractive and yet not sexualized. Her look and sound seemed to calm Jack, nothing more. "Today is Sunday, the thirtieth of October, 2067. The forecast is sunny with a light breeze from the northwest at three to four kilometers per hour. The high today is expected to be thirty-one degrees Celsius. I know, Jack. You prefer the old system. It will be eighty-eight degrees Fahrenheit. Would you like to watch the news?"

No response was possible. Jack had no memory of where he was or how he got here. He certainly had no recollection of this gadget in his hand, or even picking it up. He looked around and saw to his right a small bed. To his left was a sliding glass door that led onto a balcony. In front of him was just a sterile, white wall. "Are you all right, Jack?" There was still no answer. "Jack, should I call for an attendant?"

"Who...who...I..." All Jack could sense was confusion. Her voice was still smooth, even though the sentence seemed to convey worry. It simply added to his disorientation. He tried to swallow, but his mouth felt terribly dry. "Could you...yes...yes, please play the news...please."

"Are you sure you are all right, Jack? I sense a high degree of anxiety in your voice. Would you like to hear some music? That always puts you in a good mood. I could play some of the older songwriters you enjoy. Would you like to listen to Bruce Springsteen from the previous century? You always like Amy McDonald when you're nervous. Perhaps a Megan McGarry song from the twenties?"

"No. No music please. I'm fine."

"Would you like to continue with your reading? I can call up the collection of short stories you have been working your way through. You just finished 'Metzenger...'"

"No!" interrupted Jack tersely. He took a few heavy breaths and then said, "No. I'm sorry. Just...Please, show me what's happening. Show me the news."

"Here is today's morning broadcast. Would you like it from the beginning or in progress?"

"Just give me the live version." A beam of light suddenly shot out of the top of the handheld device. Shining on the wall in front of Jack, a picture came into view of a standard anchorman sitting behind a desk and reading a teleprompter. The old firefighter thought, *Well, at least not everything has changed.*

"...Jones Average finished down thirteen point seven today, closing out at 87,329. Now turning to local news: The top story in Pittsburgh today is the sentencing hearing for Dionysus Ankou. Testimony will be heard by the honorable Daniel Breitham. Speaking today will be the family of seven of Ankou's victims. The defense will then be given a chance to make its case for a life sentence instead of the suspended animation penalty that was approved by the jury. The defendant is expected to make a statement on his behalf. Ankou has maintained that he is a legitimate businessman, who has acquired his wealth through a long career in investments, particularly bond speculation during the market crash of '53. His lawyers still maintain that all of these charges are politically motivated."

"No. No. No," Jack began to murmur.

"The sixty-six-year-old Ankou was found guilty two months ago for ordering the deaths of multiple people over the past eleven years in an effort to consolidate his drug empire, which according to prosecutors, eventually controlled all drug trafficking in Western Pennsylvania and parts of Ohio and West Virginia. He is even reputed to control the black market cannabis cigarettes, called Ace and Amp, in the same region. Although Ankou was convicted on thirty-one counts of murder, conspiracy, racketeering, and other charges, it is speculated that he was responsible for the deaths of literally hundreds of men and women in the tri-state area over the past three decades." There was a moment of silence and the piece of glass in Jack's hand went dark. Then an advertisement came up, asking Jack if he was interested in a telecom introduction to one of the lovely senior ladies, or men, available in his area. Once it was finished the program continued. "We turn to sports with a report on the Pirates, who are looking to end their twelve-game losing streak tonight against the Vancouver Wolfpack, who are in town for a three-game series." Jack was only half listening. His mind was whirling with images, none of them dealing with sports. He decided that the last thing he remembered was the Pirates finishing another losing season, one more in a run of historic athletic incompetence. "After a promising first half of the season in the spring, the Pirates hope to recover that momentum in the autumn season in hopes of making the playoffs in December. However, the summer break seems to have had an adverse effect on their pitching. We will preview tonight's game when we return." Jack's mind dismissed the baseball talk and returned to the earlier story.

"Can you rewind that to the drug story?" It felt really odd talking to a piece of glass.

Then the young woman appeared again, and it only felt slightly strange to the old firefighter. She made it a more personal, if somewhat tenuous, interaction. "I am sorry, Jack. I do not understand what you mean by 'rewind.'"

"Could you please go back to the story about the trial of the drug dealer?"

"The sentencing hearing of Dionysus Ankou; here you are, Jack." He watched a second time, repeating the name, Dionysus, in his head again and again. Nothing was different about the broadcast, but much had changed.

The seventh time he repeated the name, something in his mind was triggered. "No. You son of a bitch. You son of a bitch, Stern!"

"What is wrong, Jack?" asked the woman from the glass card. "I sense a high degree of anger in your voice."

"Where are you Stern? Morgan!" shouted Jack. He turned back and forth, yelling at the sterile walls. "Whatever your name is...where the hell are you?"

"I am notifying the attendants, Jack. You seem to be having one of your spells." The former fireman tried to stand up, but his legs failed him. With his arms, he pushed up from the chair, but the phone or computer or whatever it was got in the way of his grip. The last thing he heard from it was, "Jack, please remain calm. The attendant has..." The woman's voice blinked out as the device hit the wall. It did not shatter, but it did break apart, finally revealing the line where the black and transparent parts are connected.

"I wonder what country is making that crap nowadays," snarled Jack. "Nowadays? What am I talking about?" He looked around again. "Where the hell am I?" Once more he began to push himself out of the chair while hollering, "Stern!" A hand came down on his shoulder and gently forced him back into his chair. Jack suddenly heard a voice singing.

The lyrics were sung in a soft, yet sad voice. The words made the pain easy to understand. His mother was dead, and his father was nearing the end as well. The singer had nobody to care for him. He had no one to love. Jack felt the complete and utter loneliness in his words and knew the lyrics were meant for him. Jack first looked at the hand on his shoulder and then followed it up to a face. "Are you all right, Mr. Lear?" It was a young, African-American man with a rounded face, bright eyes, and ears that stuck out a little too much. He wore a rumpled, brown suit and a fedora, which seemed completely incongruous with Jack's surroundings. He smiled at Jack and said, "You seem upset."

"Of course I'm upset. What the hell is going on here?" Then a thought came to Jack. This man had arrived almost instantly after the automated woman's voice said she was notifying the attendants. "You? You're not an attendant."

"No, Mr. Lear. I'm not."

"Who...what..." The disorientation had quickly returned. In frustration, Jack yelled,

"I don't belong here!"

"No sir, you don't." The man shook his head as he walked over to a small table. There was a crystalline-looking pitcher of water with a metallic filter on top. "It's hard finding yourself in a time and place that ain't yours. I know that." He poured himself a glass of water. Jack heard some ice cubes splash into the glass. "Why just a few years ago, I was visiting a time, and I heard a young girl use the term BOGO, referring to herself don't you know." He took a long drink of water. "Aahhh. Always refreshing. Nothing they come up with can replace water." The man cocked his head to the side and took a long look at Jack as if he was not sure what he had been talking about. Then he pursed his lips, shook his head once, and continued. "Now, her friend laughed, thought it was so funny that she'd be giving it up so easy if her boyfriend bought her the right things.

Imagine that...BOGO." He sighed wearily. Jack was simply dumbstruck by the matter-of-fact attitude the man had when Jack's world had been turned upside down. The young, African-American held out his hand. Jack raised his burnt hand to meet it. Without any words passing between them, Jack took the ice cube. "The ice cube takes your energy. It melts. From order comes chaos. Time goes on." Then in silence, he stared at Jack with his deep, brown eyes for a few seconds before finally saying, "Well, Mr. Lear, I'm afraid this is the end of the story, so to speak. The folks that take care of you are almost here."

Jack heard the two attendants enter the room. The woman said, "What...?" The man shouted, "Hey!" Jack's visitor in the brown suit and fedora ignored them. The young man must have had lightning in his hands, for Jack barely saw them move. The man's fist rose up and came down with a sharp crack against his temple. Jack was instantly stunned as his head snapped to the side as far as his neck muscles would allow. His eyes felt like marbles bouncing in a bag as his head whiplashed back to an upright position. Jack saw white as his vision disappeared. Then slowly the whiteness grew darker and darker.

"I don't belong..." was all he could say before the blackness overcame him.

Chapter Three

...because a quark in a proton in an atom in a shamrock

holds the Trinity.

"John Leary!" boomed a voice big enough to fill up the hollow it had been born in. The silence of the gloaming upon the hills was completely broken by, "What brings you back to Ben Nevis?" John turned around and saw a big bear of a man heading toward him. The moment John saw the man's face, the gruff voice changed from what he first thought was a challenging tone to a welcoming one. That was Father Rick's way. True, he could be loud and boisterous, but always in a friendly manner. He enjoyed life, and he wanted you to do the same. You could sense that upon meeting him for the first time. This, however, was not John's first time. The priest had been a good friend of his parents. He had been a mentor to young Johnny. Yet, John, now approaching middle- age, had not seen him in many years. The greatest truth of a small town is for it to stay small, the vast majority of its youth must move away. John had left the tiny, Pennsylvania, coal-mining town soon after graduating from the local high school in Casonville. Though he only moved a few hours away, to Butler, he had returned to his hometown only a handful of times during the intervening years.

The priest was now a few steps away, approaching fast on a stretch of cracked cement that served as the sidewalk on Main Street. John had thought of Father Rick when he parked his car, his prized Auburn 8-98 Speedster, in a small, dirt lot next to the town's one and lonely park. He had looked around at the old playground equipment, the decaying bandstand, a pavilion in need of paint, and some booths that were left from the town's Scottish Festival. It had been six years since the town had held the festival. The park did not bring back nostalgia, just a little sadness. Then he gazed at the Catholic Church where Father Rick had spent most of his career. From the steeple to the stained glass to the sanctuary, it all looked the same. Not much had changed in the years since he had last been back. John hesitated, walking past St. Timothy's, debating whether to say hello or not, but in the end, he decided to move on. What was there to talk about, even with Father Rick? No, not much had changed. Yet, he had only made it past a few row homes when he heard the low rumble of his old priest's voice.

Now it was apparent that the man was coming in for an embrace. For a moment, John felt awkward, simply due to the amount of time that had passed. That feeling quickly faded with the warm smile on Father Rick's face. That one nonverbal cue told John that all was forgiven, even the fact that John had just walked past his church without as much as a second glance. The two men hugged without saying a word. The priest patted him on the back several times before releasing him. "It's been a long time, Johnny. What good fortune to see you." The good father put his hand back on John's shoulder just to emphasize his words.

"Why's that, Father Rick?" The priest seemed to ignore the question.

"How long has it been, John?" The question made John smile, but it was to hide his confusion. Father Rick never called him John. It was always Johnny or "my son."

"Well, I guess it's been, probably...well my parents died in '29, so it's got to be six years." The math surprised John. Time had slipped away from him.

"Six years you say? You lose track. I would've bet you graduated from high school only six years ago." That made John smile, something he had not done much of in the last few years.

"Oh no. Holy cow. I graduated from Casonville in '19. C'mon Father, I've been a State trooper since '23. In fact, you are looking at the first detective ever appointed to the Butler barracks, troop D." As the sound of his voice died away, John realized that Father Rick was the first person he had told about his promotion that mattered to him. He did not have time to ponder what that meant.

"Congratulations, my son. Your parents would be so proud." John could see the look of pride in the priest's eyes as well.

"Thank you, Father. Thank you."

"No. I want to thank you, Johnny. Your family was always so supportive of my work here, particularly your dear mother. I feel indebted to folks like them." The priest paused for a moment, unsure whether he should continue, for he was intuitively aware of people's feelings. Father Rick was uncertain as to whether John would feel he was trying to top his promotion to detective. Yet, despite his long absence, John Leary was someone the priest held in great regard.

"The church has just notified me that I am to be blessed with the title of Monsignor. It appears I will be leaving old Ben Nevis after all these years. I am moving to Erie to continue my work in Bishop Gannon's office."

"That's fantastic, Father Rick, or excuse me, Monsignor Hooker. After all you have done for our town and all of Quehanna County, it is absolutely well-deserved." John smiled at the priest again.

"I would love for you to come to mass, John. I only have a few more weeks of sermons, confessions, and communion. My new duties do not include regular services, I'm afraid."

John shook his head forlornly. "I'm sorry, Father. I won't be here Sunday. Be leaving tomorrow. Got a lot of cases I'm working on. Actually, that's not true. I only have a few cases, but I'm having trouble making any progress on them. Sometimes you have to compromise your...You know...I just..." John stopped, realizing that he naturally slipped into telling his old priest what was troubling him. He was not feeling up to confessing his sins, and so he let his verbiage sputter to an end.

Father Rick saw this and offered advice instead of absolution. "You've been promoted and now you feel a lot of pressure to live up to their confidence in you."

John nodded a few times and then came clean, "Yeah. Yeah. That's it exactly."

"I know what you mean, my son. Literally. I feel the same way. But, you..." Father Rick gently poked him in the heart. "You are a talented young man. I haven't seen you in a while, but I have connections in the Pittsburgh diocese. I've heard of some of your exploits. You will be just fine, Detective Leary. However, I also know you don't attend church anymore." John dropped his head, momentarily ashamed to look Father Rick in the eye. The priest, even with all his years in the church, had never liked dealing with the subject he was about to broach. "We were all very saddened to hear of your young wife's passing. I only had the fortune to meet Angela once, but it was easy to see the love between you. I have kept her in my prayers."

John could not speak for a moment. "I'm...I'm sorry, Father. Thank you." John could muster no more words than that.

Father Rick also wanted to move on. "Ahh. But, you could come to tomorrow's mass before you leave, right? Remember, tomorrow's All-Saints Day." John went back to the false smile he had learned to use since his wife's death. The priest did not pick up on the slight differences.

"You have me there, Father. Of course, I'll come. Perhaps I'll come to confession after the mass. Will you be hearing..."

"I always have time for you, my son." He gently placed his hand back on John's shoulder and indicated that he could continue to walk as they spoke. "So, why did you say you were back in town?" John did not smile, but he finally felt some nostalgia. If Father Rick had been an old spinster, he would have been labeled a busybody or a gossip. John always wondered how he kept from crossing that line between keeping watch over his flock and truly intruding on their lives. They walked in front of the post office then crossed the street toward the Grange Hall. John paused momentarily to look at the large, tan brick meeting hall.

"My dad was always big into the Grange. I always thought it was funny cause he wasn't really a farmer. Just a cop who liked to grow berries, fruit, and such."

"Yes, but he was good at it. I always got down to Schnorr's Grocery when they had your father's fruit out. People snapped them up right away."

"Excuse me, Father. Hello. Officer Leary, I believe? How are you, sir?" They both turned around to see an older gentleman walking past a World War I marker, hurriedly approaching them in front of the Grange Hall. The man was in a full suit and tie with a hat on top of what looked like a bald head. The fedora had the houndstooth check pattern that originated in the Scottish-lowlands but had gained popularity in the United States just a few years earlier. There was a serious expression on his face, but it did not convey a negative impression. He was much shorter than John with a stocky build. "Officer Leary it is so good to see you," he said while still a good ten feet from them. There was no recognition on John's part. As the man closed the distance he said, "I thought I recognized you, walking with Father Richard." John did not remember the voice either and did not like that the approaching man knew his name. He never liked being at any kind of disadvantage.

"Father Rick, I don't know this gentleman," murmured John. There was no time for the priest to explain as the man, with a ramrod straight disposition, marched right up to them.

"Just follow my lead, son," he whispered to John.

"Could I have a word with you both?" asked the man.

"Of course, Mr. Thornton, anything for one of the devout, even if you like to follow old John Wesley's methods."

Mr. Thornton had something on his mind and did not take notice of the priest's playful prodding. He was on a serious mission. "Yes. This is not about our church. This is about our town's revival of the Ben Nevis Scottish Festival." He turned to John and said, "In addition to our celebration of the great mountain that we are named for, we hope to make it a homecoming. With that in mind, we would like to invite people from our community who have left and distinguished themselves to give a brief talk in an informal public setting, one each night. They will be feted all that day. John, I want you to be one of those speakers." He never gave John a chance to respond. "Our town needs heroes and you are one." John began to protest, but Mr. Thornton was most adamant. He went for the hard sell. "You must remember that your father was one of the organizers during our early years of having a festival." The man's visage turned sad. John thought it was due to the memory of his father, but he was wrong. "Then the war came. Now the mines are shutting down. No steel they say." Mr. Thornton looked back at Father Rick. "We must find our pride again. This town has so much to offer. Father Richard, I have heard rumors that you have been named Monsignor. I must congratulate you." The priest began to speak at what anyone would expect to be a pause, but it was not to be. "Of course, you will be one of the speakers. I know you will. Wherever that church of yours moves you to, I want you to mark off the third week of this coming June."

Father Rick was, at last, able to join the conversation. "Of course, I will. I would be honored." The man did not wait for John's affirmation, sure in the fact that he had convinced the trooper.

"All right then, I will notify the committee at the next meeting. We have four of the six nights filled. Good. Good. Have a wonderful evening, gentlemen." He shook both of their hands before the detective or the priest realized he had them in his grasp. With that, he turned away and made his way up Sixth Street.

"Do you remember him now?"

"I do. He was big into the Grange, just like my father."

"Yes." Father Rick nodded in agreement.

"I never liked him," added John.

"No?" asked the priest, surprised by the honesty

"No. He was always so stern. One time he spanked me for throwing water on another kid. We were in the basement of the hall, while they were meeting upstairs. I guess he had come down to use the toilet. Turned the corner right as I did it. Gave me a swat and told me to clean it up."

"Did you?" asked the priest despite already knowing the answer.

"Of course I did. Mr. Thornton was scary," admitted John.

Father Rick let out a bellicose laugh. "He can be stern, but he loves this community. I'll give him that." Mr. Thornton had disappeared behind the first houses above the Grange Hall's lawn.

John's attention had moved on. The son pondered the father for a moment. "Never liked going to those meetings." John did not speak for a few seconds, lost in memories. "Course if I knew then what I know now, I'd've gone to every damn one of them." Father Rick nodded knowingly. John was a tall man, but the memories were starting to bring him low. He scratched his nose and sniffed a little. Then he said, "Good food. Mom and the ladies always put together a great meal."

"Amen, Johnny. They still do, but no one makes a blueberry pie like your mom did." They turned and kept walking. A cool evening breeze blew up from the creek that ran through the lower part of town. Upon feeling it, John looked back to the south side of the borough, seeing the last remnants of the sun breaking through the bare trees on the tops of the hills. "True," answered John laconically. They had turned up Fifth Street before he spoke again. "You know she loved to go out to Briarwood Camp above Casonville and pick the wild ones there. She said they were the best. Course, my father didn't want to hear that." They turned right onto a dirt alley that ran behind the upper houses of Main Street. The gently sloping hill above them quickly turned from a mowed lawn underneath a small orchard to the neglected meadow of an abandoned property. John and Father Rick stopped and surveyed the land. Small pines had begun to grow amongst the grass. In silence they stood for several minutes. Finally, John turned to his old priest and confessed, "I'm back because I sold the property. I'll be signing off on it tomorrow in Quehanna."

Father Rick looked at him quizzically, but in the fading light John missed the unspoken question. The priest said, "I have to admit, I thought you already had. The way that section was mowed, I assumed you had sold it to Josiah Blum."

"Forgive me, Father, for I have sinned." He did not wait for the priest's usual informal response of "What troubles you, my son?" "Old man Blum wanted the land, but I never cared for him. Neither did my father. Just couldn't sell it to him. After the fire..." John stopped talking for a moment, surprised by the anger he still felt. "After it burnt down, I paid to have them cover over the foundation of the house. Then I sent money to Frank Pollard. Still do. His boy keeps that part there in the orchard, next to Fifth Street, mowed." He took a few more steps, watching the shadows of the young trees grow. "Wanted to walk up to where the house stood one more time. You wait here, Father Rick."

"Nonsense, my son." The priest moved a step ahead of him. They climbed the bank rising off the dirt road and walked up into the high grass. It took John a few minutes of stamping around, but he quickly rediscovered the foundation of his boyhood home.

He walked a few steps to his left and said, "Here's where the cellar door was." It was hard for Father Rick to see anything now, but he walked over and looked down where John was pointing. They were both focused on something so mundane that they did not see the powerful wave of danger approaching. It would have been hard to recognize it even if they had. Voices approached, young and angry voices.

"We'll get that old hag, Bennett, with these," said a teenager. A chorus of five to six adolescents expressed a variety of agreements. Without a sound, John whirled around, quickly surmised the situation, and ducked down in the high grass. The priest was about to say something to the boys when he felt John's tug pulling him down by the end of his coat.

"Get down, Father," whispered John. The priest obeyed his former charge.

Father Rick quietly asked him, "What are we doing, Johnny?"

"Just want to see what these little hoodlums are up to." At that moment, the smallest of the group, a pre-adolescent, tow-headed boy, looked in their direction. He may have heard them speaking, but did not appear to see them. The sun was now well below the hills to the southwest, and the moon had not risen yet. Darkness had come over the town with a speed only people from the hills know. The boy kept looking toward the two men but kept walking, not saying a word.

Another boy, walking beside the leader said, "I hate that old witch. Have ever since she paddled me in the third grade. Let's get her house good."

"Naw. We're gonna get her," said the tallest of them. He seemed to be in charge simply because he was the biggest. The others mumbled their acquiescence.

The kids were now far enough past John and Father Rick that the state trooper felt comfortable in giving the priest some direction. "Want to have some fun, Father, and teach them kids a lesson?" John was sure of the answer before he even formed the question.

"You know my life has been spent in an effort to save souls..." He let the statement hang in the cool, autumn air. "...by any means necessary."

"All right, they're going for Mrs. Bennett's house. She still live one house up from the corner?"

"She does," confirmed Father Rick.

"All right. You follow them. Cut off their retreat. I'm gonna go through the pines here and get ahead of them. Probably gonna mess with her house. Looked like they were carrying something. I'll wait behind that old, oak tree in her backyard and jump out right before they do. Give 'em a good scare. Any run back your way, try to corral them."

"Right." John could see a smile on the old priest's face. It brought one to his as well. With a combination of stealth and speed, John made his way through the small woods of pine. They were much taller than when he was a child, but their location had not changed. It was easy for him to beat the band of boys to Mrs. Bennett's house. Once there he crept into the yard, hoping Mrs. Bennett had not acquired a dog during the intervening years.

All seemed quiet, but John had developed a sense of the coming storm that sometimes rose in the night. It had made him an outstanding trooper. He had broken up gambling rings in Aliquippa, houses of ill repute in Mars, bootleggers in the farmlands of Zelienople, and many other lawbreakers of Western Pennsylvania. Now, he had become a detective, dealing with homicides and robberies in small towns and out-of-the-way villages that had no law of their own. This, a group of vandals, would just be a little fun. It had been a long time since he had known that feeling. In silence, he laughed to himself, hoping the surprise would go as he pictured it. John waited like a big cat, crouched behind the oak's massive trunk. He could sense the boys before he saw them. If you were quiet in body and mind, you could hear so much more. Their whispers carried farther than they ever imagined. The drag of a heel or the trip of a shoe on a stone gave them away to anyone who might be stalking them. And that was the best part for John. The little scoundrels had no idea someone was waiting for them.

"Okay, Jimmy, Tommy, and what did you say your name was?"

"Aldo," answered the small, blonde boy.

"That's a really stupid name," said the apparent leader.

"Well, my friends at my old school in Quehanna called me Al," he explained.

"Like I care. Just go with Jimmy and Tommy behind the picnic table." The one named Al just nodded, seemingly afraid of offending the older boys. "Mike and Danny, you get over there by that bush. I'm gonna knock on her back door. When she comes out, you let her have it with the eggs."

"You sure, Mark? She's kinda old," observed Mike.

"Why don't you head home, little boy. I think I hear your mama calling."

"All riiight. Give it a rest." Mike started walking toward the bush with the one named Danny. Mark headed for the back door. The other three knelt down behind the table. John could see that each of them was holding something in both hands. A quiet scrape of a patent leather shoe against a loose piece of shale on the alley's roadway told John that Father Rick had arrived. The one named Mark moved slowly down the gently sloping yard. He reached the back door and took one more look at the positions he had left his gang in. Quickly he placed one egg with the other to free up his right hand. Then he began pounding on the door. Bang! Bang! Bang! There was no reaction. Thrice more he hit the bottom of his fist against the door, slower and harder. Whump! Whump! Whump! A light came on in the kitchen. Mark stepped back and to the left, away from the rear entrance. The target was clear. A porch light came on, illuminating the yard, but not far enough to expose the vandals. The boys behind the table stood up. From behind the bush came the other two. All turned their bodies as if they were Christy Mathewson ready to pitch from the stretch. Mrs. Bennett slowly turned the knob and opened the dark-stained door. A small figure stepped out. Four right arms rose up. The one named Aldo was a southpaw. He held his more like a catcher. Mrs. Bennett took a step into the light. It was time to launch the attack.

The unseen predator leapt from a hidden ambush. "Heeeyyy! What are you doin' in my yard? Get the hell out of here! You little vandals! Who do you think you are? Get outta here before I get my salt gun!" John screamed as loud as he had ever known his voice to go. It was booming. In a moment that could not have been better timed if they had worked for weeks on the choreography, all five boys jumped, screamed, "Aaahhhhh!" and threw their eggs. Fortunately, for Mrs. Bennett, they threw them straight up into the air. Father Rick, who was expecting John's move, was still stunned enough by the ferocity of his roar that he jumped back and almost fell down. "That's it! I'm getting my shotgun. I'm gonna load it with rock salt!

See how many of you I can pepper with it!" The two boys by the bush took off toward the alley.

Father Rick stepped in front of them and stood tall. It was dark. He was a large man in black clothing. It was as if a monster had risen up in front of them. The two screamed again.

They were actually relieved when the priest's voice raged back at them. "Michael Hepburn! Danny Kildare! You little miscreants ought to be ashamed of yourselves!" Two big paws shot out and grabbed each one by the upper arm. He lifted them up until their feet had little traction. "What do you think your mothers will be saying about this?" The boys were too frightened to answer.

John had continued to terrorize the other three, but now he was confusing them. First demanding that they leave the premises immediately, now he growled like a feral beast, "Get on the ground! Get on the ground now!" The two older boys ran into each other before getting down flat on the ground. The youngest boy seemed like he already knew the drill. Before John could say, "Put your hands behind your head!" he already had. Then he knelt, but he did not lie down. John stomped the ground as he came up behind them. He stood over them, breathing heavily like a beast about to take a bite. One of the older ones was whimpering. John was pleased with his ambush, but he had forgotten one person.

From near the Bennett house came a different holler. "Hey! You don't live here! Who are you?" Mark came storming through the yard, furious that his carefully planned attack had been thwarted. "We don't have to listen to you. We don't even know you! Who do you think you are telling us..."

John was not going to listen to this for one more second. "You're about to find out," he said in a whisper as he stepped over the two boys lying on the ground. It took only three steps before the two met. Mark was a tall boy, but he was not even close to being bigger than John, who was also coming downhill at him. After the second step by John, Mark had stopped all of his momenta. The state trooper recognized this and instantly decided on his course of action. As he reached the teenager, with his third stride, the trooper jab-stepped at him and threw up his hands. Mark, who had never let go of his eggs, now jumped back with wide-eyed anticipation of what the stranger was about to do. Both hands came up in a defensive reaction, dropping the egg that was in each one. However, no attack came. With agile reflexes that shocked even Father Rick, John snatched both eggs out of the air. His hands never stopped moving. They swung up and over Mark's head. The two eggs smashed together just as the boy and man locked eyes. They kept staring at each other as first the egg whites came down, followed by the yolks. They pooled for a moment on top of his head and then ran down over the teenager's face. John did not say a word while the glutinous mess slid off Mark's chin. He simply reached out and wiped his hands on the leader of the pack's jacket.

"Let me tell you a story there tough guy," said John, loud enough for only Mark to hear with any clarity. "A few years back, before prohibition ended, I came upon a large production still, deep in the woods. Some farmer owned it. He wasn't there, but his two boys were. And they had some friends. I told 'em they were all under arrest. This one boy, he comes up to me and said, 'We ain't goin' nowhere.' He told me there was six of them and one a me. And then he said the magic words. Told me there was lots of places where they could hide the body of a state trooper and his fast car. Well, to tell the truth, I just assume he would've called my car fast, but he never actually got a chance to say the words. See, at that point my nightstick was cracking his skull...like an egg, you might say." John wiped his right hand over the boy's shoulder again. With his left hand, he grabbed the teenager's arm and pulled him in closer. Mark's eyes got even wider. John spoke in a rapid-fire manner that confused the boy even more. Every syllable was enunciated, but it was too fast for him to comprehend. It was the tone that scared him, that and John's eyes.

"Old Poison Paul Waner doesn't have a better swing than I did that day." Being a fan of the Pittsburgh Pirates, the boy did hear and understand that reference. John wanted to drive home the point a little further. "I don't mean to brag, but I got three more shots on him before his ass hit the ground. And you know what his brother and their friends did?" Mark only heard, "...you know what..." and just shook his head, hoping a negative answer was the correct one. "They got real smart. They got down on their knees and surrendered to the law. They quickly understood that the inverse of respect for the law is the pain that comes from it." Mark had no idea what the last sentence meant. All he understood was the resonance of John's voice when he said the word, pain. "That moonshiner spent the next six months in and out of hospitals. I'm told he sits on the porch a lot nowadays, listening to the birds." While Mark swallowed hard and imagined an invalid on a porch, John turned around and stared at the three behind him. They had been looking up, but the instant John turned around the two prone boys buried their faces in the grass. The one called Al just smiled. John turned back around but made a mental note to check out the identity of that one. "You got any idea how mad my commander was?" The boy whimpered a little.

"Not mad at all, not one bit. He just shook my hand and thanked me. Told me the man should've known better than to threaten a trooper." John let that thought sink in for a few seconds. "That was the last man that told me I had no authority." John paused for effect. Then he growled, "Till you." Mark tried to speak, but could not make his voice work. "Now you want to save face with your buddies," whispered John. "So, you just lead them out of town. Don't let me catch you vandalizing or tormenting anyone else tonight. You got that?" The teenager nodded profusely, and John let his arm go. The boy backed away but kept staring at him. John nodded once toward the south to let him know that he should get on with it.

"C'mon...c'mon guys. Let's get out of here. My brother told me they're having a dance up in the barn at the Curry farm." The other three were not moving.

John recognized this and took a deep breath. "Get out of here!" he roared. In a flash, they were on their feet and following Mark again. John turned to where

Father Rick was standing with the other two vandals still firmly in his grasp. "It's all right, Father. You can let them go. I think they just want to go find some cute girls to dance with."

"So be it," growled the priest. "But don't think I won't be talking to your parents about this before I go." The other two quickly stepped away from him and got to the relative comfort of their little band. They scurried down the remainder of the alley. John and Father Rick watched them hit the main road from Casonville, cross over, and head south toward Caledonia with great haste. As he watched them disappear into the shadows, John's mind turned to another peculiarity. Mrs. Bennett was still standing on her back porch. He now realized she had not said a word. Nor had she shown any fear, at least none that he had noticed. There were no screams or fainting spells or anything. He continued his walk through the yard.

"Mrs. Bennett, are you all right?" There was no response. "Mrs. Bennett, my name is John Leary. I grew up on Fifth Street." He pointed back the way he had come. "I'm a state trooper now ma'am." He stepped onto her porch. Her eyes had followed him, but she did not say anything. "I hope I haven't caused you any trouble, Mrs. Bennett. I was just trying to stop those boys from doing any vandalism to your..."

"She says the man of the ring waits for you," interrupted Mrs. Bennett in a monotone. With slightly more emotion, she fixed her eyes on John's and said, "The, the light must not be his." John leaned in a little, reflexively thinking that if he was closer he might understand her better. The woman continued, "If, if the girl in Coombe Abbey is freed, no one will stand against the fascists." Then she turned around, opened the door, and walked back into her house. John heard the door being locked and the kitchen light went out. He stared at the door for a few moments, unsure of what to do.

Once his eyes adjusted to the darkness, he turned around and asked, "Did you hear that?" He did not honestly think that his priest had, but he was so confused he asked anyway.

"Yes," was all Father Rick could say. He was replaying her words in his mind, trying to make sense of them.

"What was that about? I mean she didn't have to thank us, but…"

The priest could not understand the content, so he turned his reasoning to the messenger. "My son, I'm afraid Mrs. Bennett has become a bit doddering since she retired from teaching. Sometimes she gets confused. She probably has read something or heard something on the radio about what's going on in Europe."

"Oh." John still felt it to be strange, but shrugged his shoulders and let it pass. He stared to the south, in the direction the boys had gone for a few seconds. Then he turned back to Mrs. Bennett's door for a few more. Finally, he walked over to Father Rick. "Let's walk down here toward the intersection. Someone told me the big town of Ben Nevis actually has a traffic light." They began following in the footsteps of the mischief-makers.

"Yes indeed." Father Rick's smile beamed, for he was glad to be distracted from Mrs. Bennet, but John did not see it in the growing darkness. "We are now a metropolis on par with Casonville and one traffic signal behind Quehanna." They walked past the only garage in town and stopped on the corner just to stare at the device.

"Forgive me father, but my hometown, like most of the country, doesn't seem very prosperous right now. How is it we can afford a traffic signal."

"Well, it depends on two things, tragedy and influence. The short answer is the state paid for it. The long answer is several people were killed at this intersection because of cars rambling through here. This route connects Quehanna with Indiana and no one thinks to slow down for our small town. One of the victims was related to our state senator. A few months later we..."

"Help! Father Rick, please help!"

The two men turned around to see a dark-haired woman coming down the street, keeping a slow running pace. She was wearing a plain skirt and a light jacket. As she approached, John thought that she looked like someone who had once been pretty. He quickly realized it was an unfriendly and, for some unknown reason, a discomfiting thought. Wondering why it had come to his mind, he kept silent.

"What is it child," asked Father Rick. "What's wrong?" She was close enough to now see a few details in the low light of the garage's sign and the traffic light. The woman stared at John for just a second. It was enough for him to recognize that life had beaten her down a few times too many, but that was all he saw for the moment. As he first suspected, she appeared not homely but worn thin. The woman ignored his looks of curiosity and pity; turning to the person she thought might assist her. "Have you seen a gang of teenagers?" she said, answering the priest's question with her own desperate one. As she spoke, she took one step closer to Father Rick. That was one more step out of the shadows. In that brief moment of time, John understood both what the woman was and the effects that alcohol can have. An identity had almost been reached, but how slowly the analysis was coming together frustrated John's investigative mind. There were crow's feet around her eyes, but it was the blood vessels below them that gave away the self-medication the woman administered. A lot of damage appeared on her cheeks. He could also see it in her reddish nose and bloodshot eyes. It appeared that this woman had enjoyed more than her share of cocktails. That was not exactly accurate. No, nothing so fancy as a mixed drink with a silly name; whiskey was her poison.

The woman looked to be much older than John, but something had been tugging at his mind all along. In turning away, he recognized the profile with its pertly-shaped nose and delicate lips. She had once been so beautiful to him. There were moments, terrible moments during those sleepless nights after his wife's passing when he had wished more than anything that he had stayed in Quehanna County and made a life with this woman instead. He would have avoided all the pain. Come the light of day, when he stared at the rising sun, all of that disappeared and he just missed his wife.

If he could only see her smile one more time, his days would have more meaning. His nights would not be so dark. Work would seem less important. It would not be the driving force in his life. However, that was not going to happen, and John had come to that realization long before he saw his childhood sweetheart looking so very less than radiant.

"Lana? Lana Sachsen." Even though it had come slowly to him, John subconsciously expected quick recognition from her. They had dated for two years. It went unsaid, even in his thoughts, but John knew he did not look as worn out as she did. More importantly, he expected her to now ask him for help. John was an officer of the law and a man who, according to many people, looked like he could get things done.

"I'm sorry, sir. I need to talk to Father Rick." John turned to Father Rick as if to ask how it was possible she did not realize who he was. The reverend was listening intently. "These teenagers, these kids, they..."

"Yes, dear. We just chased them out of town. John here scared the living daylights out of them." The name made something click in her head. Both John and Father Rick saw the lightbulb come on. Unfortunately, it was not a bright and shiny light.

"John Leary!" She turned back to him. "John Leary!" She punched him right in the chest. "Ain't you supposed to be some kind of cop?"

John was not hurt, but he was stunned. With a devastating quickness, it became apparent to him that they were not going to have a cheery reunion. It seemed she did not hold memories of him in quite the same esteem as he did of her. "Yeah. Yes. I'm a detective with the state police."

"Well, why the hell did you let 'em go?"

"Because they hadn't done anything serious." John was moving past his initial surprise and was becoming agitated. He did not care to be addressed with such rudeness no matter who was doing it.

"No? No?" She took a breath, appearing to wrestle with her anger, unable to even think straight. "I put up with stealing my chickens one year and lettin' em loose in the school. I didn't do anything last year when they somehow put our wagon on top of the barn!" She turned to Father Rick and said, "Probly cause it made Greg have to actually do some work." Her bloodshot eyes zeroed back in on John, who was trying to decide if he had ever met Greg. "Now they've went too far. They set fire to the barn! Who knows what would've happened if I hadn't come home from my mom's place cause I'd forgot the apples!" She was on the verge of shouting now. Tears were streaming down her face.

"Whoa. Whoa. Lana, hold on."

"No! I'm not gonna hold on. I'm tired of working all the time and getting nothing for it. I'm tired of this whole damn town! You're supposed to be a cop! I want them boys arrested! I want them..."

"Okay. Okay. I'll find 'em," he assured her.

"Find 'em and arrest 'em!" she hollered.

"I will. I'll..." Boom! John immediately stopped talking and spun around. It was not close, but he quickly recognized the sound of a firearm. From the full-throated echo of the shot, he figured it for a shotgun, perhaps as big as a ten gauge. Looking beyond the hardware store on the opposite corner, John knew he was not going to see anything. The sound of the weapon came from that direction though. He did not need to be a police officer for his instincts to tell him that on this night the sound of a gun meant trouble. Boom! As though he had asked for confirmation, another shot rang out. At a jogging pace, he crossed the intersection and headed toward the railroad tracks, leaving Lana and Father Rick in stunned silence. The hoodlums, who were apparently more dangerous than John thought, had gone this way. It was an easy bet that they were involved. He turned right and headed up Coal Hill. His pace quickened as he went past the Caledonia tipple and down the road toward the first farm on the south side of town. A trickle of sweat ran down his temple. It felt cold and out of place in the night air.

Rounding a sparse copse of pine trees, John slowed to a range walk and pulled his .32 caliber, standard-issue Colt revolver from inside his jacket, hoping it would not be needed. Upon turning the corner, he gripped the pistol just a little tighter. What he saw meant danger was waiting. It was not just a drunk firing his shotgun into the air like some expensive noisemaker. There beyond the trees that lined the road heading toward a barn, he could see a small fire burning. He heard voices, desperate voices, but could not see the people they belonged to just yet. "Please. Please don't shoot me. Please."

"You shut up! You just shut up! You think you can..."

"I didn't...I didn't do any..."

John slid quietly past the last tree and into the yard in front of the farmhouse. He went into a fighter's crouch and took aim before speaking. There was more than a fair chance a gun barrel would be the response to his command. What he saw before him was disturbing, even for an experienced policeman. The boys he had scared less than a half-hour before were now in almost the same position. Only this was much more serious than a cop having some fun with them. The one named Danny was face down on the right wheel lane of the road. John could see a dark spot growing in the dirt underneath him. Tommy was farther to the right; the closest one to what John now realized was a feeding trough on fire. He was also down and not moving. The other four were on their knees, shaking and crying. Mark had a double barrel in his face.

An old man stood over them. It was someone John did not recognize. For a brief moment, he tried to remember who owned this farm when he was a kid, but realized it meant little even if he could. The immediate concern was the man with the gun. Two shots had been fired, but it was apparent that if they had come from that shotgun, it had been reloaded. Mark had his hands out in front of him in a reflexive defensive position, too scared to understand that it would do little good. In the light of the burning trough, it was easy to see that the old man's face was a collage of reds and purples. Veins bulged in his neck. John's eyes bore in on his right hand, the trigger finger held tense. "You dirty little bastards! I've had it with you!" John carefully and quietly took two more steps.

"I swear, Mister. We didn't..."

"Shut your mouth, you little punk!" In hollering at the boy, the man had swung the barrels of the shotgun away from Mark's face. John saw that this was his chance to get the man's attention without him accidentally shooting Mark in the head.

"Put the gun down," yelled John with a resonance of authority. The gun did not go down. Instead, it came up, but John did not fire. The aged man clearly did not see him, for he only pointed the gun in John's general direction, and would have missed by a mile even with a shotgun's spread of pellets. "I am a state police trooper! Detective John Leary! Put the gun down, sir, and back away. This doesn't have to get any worse!" The gun swung back a little and was now pointing toward John. Still, the trooper held his fire. Mark ducked down, prostrated before the crazed old man. The farmer's eyes burned with the reflected light of the small fire, and even though he looked and moved as if ancient, the man had been so unpredictable, twitching and fuming, that he seemed to be a living cloud of chaos. Confusion reigned, which made John all the more cautious. What would make him shoot another child? That was the overriding thought as John moved closer. The more he closed the range between them, the better chance of an accurate shot from the .32 revolver. "Put the gun down, sir. This is over."

"The hell it is. I'm not gonna take it anymore. These little punks have been tormenting me for years. Rocks through my windows. Tearing up my fields. Lettin' loose my animals. They set fire to the hay in my feed trough. I coulda taken all that, but they killed my dog. My dog, damn it! They killed my dog!"

"Sir, we will find out who killed your dog. These boys are in trouble for other things, but you can't take the law into your own hands." The two men stared at each other, looking for the first sign of aggression. The boys had begun to watch them. Their eyes darted back and forth between the two weapons. "We will find who did this, but these boys couldn't possibly be doing all the vandalism in this town. They're not that fast. Now we can save this situation if you just put the gun down."

"I swear we didn't kill anyone's dog, mister!" cried the one named Mike.

"You shut up you little bastard! You're lying! Nothin' but lies, just like he lied to me...back when...back..." The confusion of the situation had begun to infect his mind, or perhaps it had sprung from there.

In the calmest voice he could manage, John continued. "Put the gun down, sir. I want to find out who killed your dog, but I can't do that if..."

"You can't save my dog. And you can't save me."

"I'm not gonna lie to you, sir. You're in serious trouble here. But I don't know the whole story. Put that gun down and let's get to the bottom of it." John stopped moving. He was within a range that he knew a kill shot was certain. The man's histrionics paused long enough for John to hear people approaching from behind him. He quickly decided that it was Father Rick and Lana. Confirmation was out of the question. It would mean taking his eyes off the old man and his shotgun. John knew that a fraction of a second would be all the reaction time he would have if the man decided to fire again, either at him or another boy. His mind quickly processed the information in his subconscious, and he concluded that the farmer was alone in his madness. The running footsteps did not belong to any co-conspirators. Sure enough, Lana and Father Rick arrived at John's side and immediately announced their presence.

Breathlessly, the priest began to say, "Mr. Rotz, what are you..." But he was interrupted by the horrified scream that came from Lana once her brain finally made sense of the bizarre and grisly scene in front of her. Without thinking she hurried to the side of the nearest victim.

"Lana, wait!" came too late from John, but it would not have stopped her anyway. The detective kept his pistol aimed at the center mass of the man.

"What have you done? What have you done?" yelled Lana.

"They had it comin'! They had it comin'!" hollered Rotz back at her. "They killed my dog! Why'd they have to go and kill my dog?" The man had turned his head, and John almost took the shot, but as the shotgun's barrels swung back and forth with his gesticulations, Mark began to move about to get away from the business end of the gun. The boy's movement was enough to keep John from firing. His training told him that even though he had a clear line of fire, it was not clear if a bystander could move in front of the shot at the same moment he decided to pull the trigger.

"Oh, God! Oh no," cried Lana as she turned over Danny's body. His eyes looked dull and lifeless in the flickering light of the burning trough.

"Mr. Rotz, please put down the gun," implored Father Rick.

At the same time, Mark began to bawl. "I want my mother! I want my mother!" he cried, but there was no one able to comfort him.

"No. No. No," Lana kept repeating as she slid over to Tommy, who was also motionless It was easy to see that he had died almost instantly. He had taken a blast of buckshot squarely in the chest.

Father Rick suddenly lost interest in the standoff. The first thing he had noticed was Mr. Rotz with the gun, and his instincts were to mediate the confrontation. Now he saw the devastation the gun had wrought. The priest walked right in front of John's barrel. With growing exhaustion, he knelt at the side of Danny Kildare. The Father's voice was cracking as he began to recite the Commendation of the Dying, "Per istam sanctan unctionem et suam piissimam misericordiam, indulgeat tibi Dominus..."

John stood in a crouched stance. His firearm was motionless without even the slightest tremble. He was one of those rare individuals, who in a time of crisis did not become agitated. His heart rate remained calm. Sometimes it even slowed down. Things on the periphery disappeared. Even when Father Rick passed in front of him, John did not move or break his concentration. All of the growing bedlam was processed by his brain, but it did not upset or disturb John. He knew the situation was growing out of control. It had to end before another innocent person got hurt. John had to give the man one last chance, but that would be it. "Sir, I am ordering you to put down the weapon and slowly move away from it. If you do not comply..."

"Officer Leary. Officer Leary." It was the boy named Aldo. He was kneeling on the ground, facing away from John. Now he turned around and looked at the trooper with the sweetest smile on his face. A battle raging around him would have no effect, but somehow, this kid's voice and smile were enough to break John's concentration. The policeman glanced at the boy, who was slightly to his left. The blonde hair framed a face that could only be described as cherubic. With great speed, John's eyes came back to Rotz, but the boy still claimed some of his attention.

"What do you want, son?" The boy had unnerved John, but he had also silenced the old man, Rotz.

"Officer John Leary; barracks D out of Butler County." The strangeness of the statement made even Rotz look at the child.

"Stay still and be quiet boy!" said John emphatically.

"Tell me Officer Leary, if Jackson had been with Lee would they have won at Gettysburg? Would they have won the battle that came later?" John's focus completely broke and he turned to look at the child.

"What are you..." John never got to finish his question. And he never saw the young boy again.

"You! I shoulda killed you before! I don't know how you...you...Damn you! Too young then...I...I...Goddamn you, I shoulda killed you, you bastard!" Any sense of control Rotz might have had was now gone. "You're a demon just like the rest! You're a demon! Let's finish this!" he screamed. The barrels of the old farmer's gun were raised and pointed directly at John. There was no time to negotiate. There was not even time to think. The muscles in John's arms tensed for control, and he squeezed the trigger three times in rapid succession. All three shots hit the man, but there was no chance for a tight shot group. As John had pulled the trigger on the second shot, Farmer Rotz had reflexively pulled the front trigger on his double barrel. It exploded to life as if a dragon had suddenly belched. John felt the impact of the buckshot tearing into his left hip as he fired the .32 caliber pistol for the third time. It staggered him, but only four of the shot penetrated deeply. Two more ripped through the flesh of his side. The rest of the shotgun's blast missed completely. John dropped to his knees, twisting in agony, yet never losing sight of Rotz. The old man fell straight back with two bullets in his chest and another lodged in his left shoulder. His gun pointed straight to the sky but was still held firmly in his grasp.

"Johnny!" yelled Father Rick and Lana at the same time. The old priest stood up and rushed toward John, who had lowered his pistol but continued to stare at the old man's body. Mark dove to the right, holding his hands over his ears with his eyes tightly shut. The two other boys, Jimmy and Mike, got up and ran. Not bothering to find a road or trail, they ran straight through a thicket of thorns and underbrush, tearing their clothes and skin.

Just as the good Father reached John's side and said, "How bad is it, son?" they all heard an unnatural, guttural scream come from the old man.

He sat up and roared, "Die you goddamn, nigger-lovin' Quaker!" Lana, who was a few steps behind the priest, shrieked in absolute terror, for despite having only one shot left, she was sure he would kill them all. Father Rick began to step in front of John in a brave act of selflessness. The state trooper brought the revolver up and aimed it at the notch where the old farmer's brow, eyes, and nose met, but with Father Rick drawing closer, he only used his left hand to hold the weapon, trying to push the priest aside with his right. The farmer pulled the second trigger on the shotgun. At the same instant, John squeezed off another round from the pistol. Buckshot tore into Father Rick's upper thigh, taking him to the ground. Several pieces of shot slammed into John, shattering his collarbone, but luckily missing his neck and its vital arteries and veins. He tumbled over backward and dropped his sidearm. It hit with a heavy thud. The bullet that had just left its barrel did not find its intended target. John missed badly but still managed to hit the man for a fourth time. Instead of a kill shot, the piece of lead gashed a hole in Rotz's side, smashing a rib, ricocheting, and slashing through the man's liver. It came to rest above his pancreas. Rotz's upper body began to twist from the torque provided by the bullet, but with his legs on the ground, he could not go anywhere. Out of options, his body just fell to the side. With blood running from his mouth and nose and a blank expression in his eyes, the old man stared at John, Father Rick, and Lana. The life seemed to drain from him, soaking into the ground. Lana knelt between the two men who had been wounded.

"Oh, God! Oh, God! What do I do? What can I do?"

John blindly reached up with his right hand and grabbed her arm. He could only bend the arm at the elbow, for his shoulder had been destroyed. "Lana..." It hurt to even speak. Every movement of his neck or jaw radiated pain through the broken collarbone. "Lana...go into the old man's house. Get some clean towels or sheets if you can find 'em. I need to...I need you to dress these..." John's sight came back for a second and then blacked out again. A disturbing pang from his destroyed trapezius muscles shot down his spine and collaborated with the throbbing pain in his pelvis. The combined stimulus almost made him go into shock and pass out. He gritted his teeth hard enough that when he swallowed a little saliva, some enamel went down his throat as well. "Aaahhh." His vision cleared and he spoke again. "Once you get that, you need to find the nearest house with a phone. Mmmmm. Call, or ask the operator to connect...connect you to the Quehanna police...or the state police barracks in

Holzfaller. Mmmm." He clenched his teeth again.

"Okay. Okay. Okay." Lana stood up, but kept staring at John, not moving.

"Go!" demanded John.

"Okay, but Father Rick?"

"I...I am fine, my child," assured Father Rick. "Go. Go get help." Without another word, Lana ran for the farmhouse. For a few seconds, there was stillness as the sound of her footsteps faded. Even Mark was quiet, for he was too scared to move or even speak. Though not physically hurt, he was falling into shock just as much as John was. Father Rick lay on his good side, breathing heavily. In a whispered voice, John heard him reciting the twenty-third Psalm. John looked straight up into the sky. Then something caught his eye. He turned his head and saw a full moon just beginning to rise over Simpson's Hill, but he could only look for the briefest of moments. When he turned his head the stinging agony of his broken collarbone made him snap back to a position looking straight up. For a few seconds, he moaned in agony. Then he tried to gain some control. Wracked with pain, he clenched his teeth tightly together again and became silent. It was then that he heard the voice. So quiet at first that John dismissed it as a hallucination generated by his own pulsating nerves.

"Father? Father Richard?" A sense of disbelief came over John. This was quickly replaced with shocked resignation. With his left hand, he began to blindly reach for where he thought he had dropped his gun. "Father, please help me. Before I die...please...please hear me." John swallowed hard and squeezed his eyes shut in the vain hope that it would affect his hearing also. The old man Rotz could not possibly be alive. "Father, I don't want to die...I know he's waiting for...for me." It was then that John heard the priest begin to crawl away from him.

"Father Rick...don't..." was all John could say.

"I must." The priest slowly drew closer to Rotz. He heard fear in a voice reciting a prayer he was familiar with. It was mixed with a deathly gurgling.

"My God, I'm heartily sorry for offending you. I detest my sins, which..." Coughing erupted. Father Rick crawled a few more feet. "...because of your justice, but more because you are God. You are all good." Father Rick was almost beside him. Both John and Father

Rick could hear him spitting up blood. Still, the man continued. "You deserve all of my love."

He coughed a few more times. "Father? Father, is that you? Forgive me, Father..."

"I don't think we have time to deal in formalities. Confess your sins, Herman Rotz. It is Herman, right?"

"It is." A wheeze followed the statement, along with fluids. Rotz tried to gather his thoughts, but the blood loss was forcing his body to start shutting down. It was getting harder to form a coherent idea. "I'm not quite sure how I...I got here. But, but I know...this is..."

He coughed again, and Father Rick was now close enough to be hit by some of the frothy blood from his mouth. The wheezing was growing louder as both of his lungs began to collapse. "He said I owed him my life. And he was right. Tried to run. Tried to hide from him. Ended up here. No hiding from my sins." He coughed a few more times. "Found me. Said we'd be even if...if I burnt it down." Father Rick had seen this fear a few times before. John had not. The dying man, or woman, started rambling, hoping to get it all out before their last breath. The priest tried to focus on the man. John tried his best to ignore the pain and listen to his words.

"Who told you? Who found you, Herman?" asked the priest.

The old farmer ignored the questions. "I didn't know Father. Didn't know they was home and in bed. Told me it was empty. I'm a...I've done some bad things, but...but I didn't want to kill those...that nice couple. Forgive me. He's waiting, Father. Oh, God forgive..." A last gurgling breath escaped what was left of his lungs. Though he was gone, his words now did more damage than his shotgun had. It was a small town, and it did not take long for John and Father Rick to realize what the man was confessing. It hit Father Rick like a sledgehammer to the chest. John's emotions spun out of control, but his body was paralyzed with pain. Father Rick, now officially Monsignor Richard Hooker, felt like he could not breathe, but he remained selfless, waving Lana past him and onward to John. Lana did not realize what was happening to Father Rick and followed the motions of a man she had always respected. Except for marrying her deadbeat husband, who was not a Catholic, she had always listened to Father Rick, and that is why she carried an armful of ripped-up sheets past him to use on John first.

Coming close to hitting him, she slid in beside her former beau. "Tell me what to do,

Johnny. Tell me what to do. I don't know what to do with gunshots."

John ignored her. Somehow, despite the old man's dying whisper of a voice, John had been able to hear every word. He could not tell how bad his wounds were, but they did not hurt as much as they once did. Clarity had come to him, and it was welcome. A revelation had been bestowed. Yet, physically, all John knew was that he was cold and sleepy. Before he could close his eyes, before he could slip away, John needed, above anything else, confirmation. "Lana?"

"Yeah, Johnny. Tell me what to do."

"Did I kill the man who killed them? Killed my...my parents...and me? Is he dead?"

Lana dropped the sheets and grabbed John's face. She stroked his hair and caressed his cheek, understanding clearly what was happening. "No. No. I won't let you...you're not going to..." John heard nothing more. He closed his eyes.

Chapter Sixteen

...because it is said to be sweet for a young girl.

Jack heard the footsteps. They moved very slowly in the hay. Someone was carefully sneaking up on him. He had felt their presence a few times before and had wondered when they would make their move. Now, the approach was unmistakable. It would be today. Despite thinking about this moment for a long time, Jack still did not know how he would respond. Should he surprise them or wait for their move and react to it? He was growing nervous. How far away were they? It was hard to judge simply by the sound of a light rustle in the grass. Patience was not a virtue in Jack's eyes. Simply waiting on things to unfold was almost unbearable for him. As he listened, goosebumps raised on his arms, and tingles went down his spine, all driven by the nervous energy flowing through him. It jumped with every soft footfall or brush through the waving grass. There it was, almost imperceptible, but it could not be misheard. A small twig had snapped, and then there was the movement of the grass right after it. The mysterious presence had known instantly that they had made a mistake and reacted by instinctively moving backwards.

As if it was meant to torture poor Jack, the wind blew across the field with a strong breeze. He did not dare tip his hand, continuing to eat the lunch he had brought. For a couple of minutes there was only silence, but for the chomping and grinding of the cattle obliviously feeding, while Jack waited patiently for his destiny to play out. It was when the wind, a gentler breeze, changed direction that he knew he had been bested. Their scent was now directed toward Jack's nose, and he suddenly realized that this presence he had felt previously was standing right behind him. Before he could change his mind and take control of the situation, hands shot out toward his head and grasped him.

They covered Jack's eyes, but the man did not get up from his lunch. He merely swallowed, wondering how much his reaction had been noticed. Jack felt a shift in weight and then sensed their lips very close to his right ear. A few warm breaths fell on the lobe, eliciting raised hairs on his neck. In a soft whisper he heard, "I've been watching you."

Jack was not sure how to respond. He desperately wanted to get it right. "I know," was all he could come up with. The hands did not move, but they did pull back a little.

"How could you?" The voice made his head tingle, and he felt a light sensation roll down his spine. This time Jack recovered with a much better response.

"It's hard not to notice the most beautiful girl you've ever seen; even when she is trying to hide from you."

"That, Dear Jack, was almost perfect."

"Almost?"

"I am a woman, not a little girl."

"Yes, you are. You are the beautiful woman with no name who haunts my dreams."

She released her hands from his eyes and walked a few steps to be in front of him.

With a lovely graceful movement, she was suddenly kneeling on the blanket he had spread out. "I told you that you would see me again." She was playful. It was one of the many things that drew Jack to her. He was desperate to keep it going.

"So, is this just one more dream? Will I ever see you again for real?"

"Who's to say if this is real, but you are not sleeping. You are, however, a silly man." Jack was momentarily speechless, spellbound by her eyes and smile. She effortlessly shifted the direction of their conversation. "Then again, this could be a dream. I've never heard tell of a man who watches cattle, spreading out a blanket at the edge of the field and sitting down to a nice lunch. You are quite different, Jack. I find you most fascinating."

"Thank you..." He had paused in the hopes that she would offer her name, but it was not forthcoming. She had other things on her mind.

"What do you call it?"

"I...aahh...I just call this bread. I don't think it has a special name." She laughed at his answer and just as fast he regretted saying it. Hearing his own voice saying the words was painful, for it sounded as dumb to Jack as it must have to the lovely woman before him.

A smaller smile came over her face. It softened from a playful glee to compassion. Suddenly, Jack felt safe. "I do not mean that, Jack," she said softly. "I mean this meal you have been enjoying at this time for the past three days."

"Oh, I see." He was torn. The compassion she had shown with just a facial expression made Jack's heart melt, but at the same time, he knew that he did not want to appear to need that same emotion. Somehow, at this point, silliness was safer.

"Pardon me, my lady, but it was bait?"

"Bait?" The lady was quite confused and perhaps a little offended.

"Oh, yes. I was trying to lure in a most exquisite creature."

"And what do you call this, this bait?" Jack removed a glass jar of jam from his knapsack. With his knife, he spread a little on a piece already cut from the loaf of bread he had brought. Before answering her, he handed the piece of bread to the young woman and indicated she should try it. The mystery girl accepted and took a cautious bite, keeping her eyes on Jack the whole time. "That's delicious. It tastes so fresh."

"My aunt was kind enough to give me some when she last cooked up the grapes. She uses beet sugar. Says the recipe and process goes back hundreds of years. What she told me is that a grandfather, many generations ago, brought it back from the crusades against the

Saracens. How's that for a story?"

"I love a good story," she confirmed.

"I know. You told me."

"But, I must admit, I do not know what a crusade or a Saracen is?" She seemed to mimic a sheepish look.

"Well, that's a good question. I think it was some type of war that a lot of people went off to fight. You know, like King Richard the Lionheart."

"My mother told me stories of him. What's a Saracen?"

"People in the Orient I think."

"Oh, so those that live in the East are called Saracens? I thought they were called Turks." She gave Jack a quizzical look.

"You know I have to tell you...and I don't like admitting this to anyone...I have no idea." He laughed at himself, but did not mind when she joined in.

"Well, aren't we two dullards," declared the maiden.

"Yes, we are. I just heard my uncle call another one of his workers a mome. I thought it was a funny word. I think it means the same thing, you know, a fool." He smiled, thinking he might have impressed her, despite his lack of education.

"Mome? I will have to remember that one." A momentary silence fell over them.

"Jack?" She smiled as she as she asked and Jack's eyes brightened even more.

"Yes?" His eagerness almost made him mispronounce a one-syllable word.

"What were we talking about?" They laughed together, then both said, "Two momes!" and laughed some more.

Once they had stopped giggling, Jack answered her. "I think you asked me what I called this." He waved his hand over the blanket and food and drink. "It doesn't have a name as far as I know. It's just a meal. Probably should have a name, something pretty or fun. You'd be a good one to think of its name," said Jack, trying to motivate more conversation.

She smiled again. They both were full of smiles. Before she could say anything, that one realization came to her. It was nice to smile and laugh with someone so much. "I'm afraid I'm not smart enough to come up with new words, but my mother always told me that we like to steal words from other people."

"Really? Like who?"

"Like the Romans. The Germans. The French." Her eyes got a little wider and she became even more animated. "That's who could name something like this, the French. Sitting in a meadow, eating a meal, when you're supposed to be working, Jack; that's something the French would do." Jack immediately scanned the field on the other side of the stream they were sitting close to. He rapidly counted the cattle and exhaled a deep breath when he got to the total he needed. "At least that's what my mother tells me." Jack was not listening to her last statement, concentrating on the grazing bovines.

"They are just fine." He pointed to the white, long-horned cattle. Then he looked at her seriously for a moment. "Why didn't you come over before today?"

"I wasn't sure what you were after. I thought I would just watch you for a while."

Jack had reached the limits of his vocabulary and did not know how to continue the back and forth. He changed direction. "I know you watched me. It was all I could do to not yell an invitation across the field." Jack wanted information, but was interrupted first.

"Why didn't you?" she asked with an air nonchalance.

"Why didn't I what?"

"Yell out an invitation," she said as if it was so obvious.

"Because I wanted you to come down to the stream on your own accord. I wanted to know you were curious. I needed to know if you wanted to see me."

"And now you have captured your quarry."

"No. You're not that."

"Really? Then what type of prize did you yearn for?"

"Wait. No. I don't mean that. You were the prize, but you see...I don't want you to think that I think you are just something I can capture. I just...umm..." She let him squirm a little longer before rescuing him.

"Don't worry, silly. I understand. It's nice to be wanted, especially if it means I get some more of this grape jelly. It's tart and sweet at the same time." Jack obliged, feeling relieved that she was not mad at his verbal faux pas. They took the time to eat a few bites. Jack briefly stood up and looked over his uncle's cattle, more to figure out what he should say next than to get a headcount.

"So how long are you going to tease me?" asked Jack with a false sense of seriousness.

The young woman misread the tone and believed him to be challenging her. "I don't know that I have ever teased you. Whatever are you talking about?"

Jack gave her a look that conveyed, "Really? Are you daft?" but instead he simply said, "You know I could easily go to town and ask around. I'm sure someone would tell me your name." She now understood that he was trying to be playful with her once more.

"And in your efforts to discover my identity, how would you describe me to the townsfolk? Some foolish girl who wanders around the meadows to the north of town?"

"No. Although, if you think about it, that is not a bad description." They both chuckled a little because it was true. "No. I would say she is about sixteen and a half hands, probably nine stone."

She gave him a spirited punch in the chest and with mock indignation exclaimed, "I'm not one of your horses or precious cattle!" He acted hurt, but could not contain his laughter.

Then a serious look came over Jack's face. "Actually, what I would ask them is, 'Do you know a girl with hair prettier than a field of sunflowers in summer? Have you seen her eyes, those that shine brighter than the Queen's jewels, and her smile whiter than fresh snow? She's a woman whose shadow could make a man sweat on a cold, winter day. I am sure you would remember her, because her beauty haunts your memories.'" They looked into each other's eyes for a few moments, hoping the spell would last. However, words only carry a little bit of magic.

"I am afraid it is you who are now teasing." She pursed her lips, but not in anger. It was as if she wanted to say more, but was trying to hold it back.

"You are wrong, my friend. What I say is true. The maiden most fair, soever in all the land." All of what Jack had said was winning her over. He would have been relieved to know it. The anxiety he felt with each sentence was unbearable. It was a constant battle to avoid saying something stupid or offensive or just plain boring. He also would have been surprised to know that of all the things he had said, calling her "my friend" had made the most impact. It had caught her off guard. She was surprised by the emotion she felt. It made her nervous for the first time in as long as she could remember. That made her uncomfortable and she quickly planned her exit. Perhaps this was moving too fast, but she also wanted it to continue. She got to her feet.

"Have I offended you?" asked Jack earnestly. "I wasn't teasing."

"No. I wasn't offended, Jack." She smiled warmly at him and then knelt down. He moved, as fast as he could, from a seated position to a kneeling one. They faced each other in silence for a few moments before she reached out and caressed his cheek. Then she leaned in toward him. "This is teasing," she whispered in his right ear. Her lips gently brushed against his cheek, kissing him ever so lightly. She moved around to the other side of his face, slightly touching his nose with hers. In his left ear she breathed, "This is me yelling an invitation." Every hair on Jack's head and neck and arms were standing on end. He felt more than tingles in his spine. They exploded in an electrical shiver as her lips pressed against his. He closed his eyes, afraid that if he observed what was happening it would disappear. All over his body, he felt a lightness envelop him. There was an urging within him that he knew he could not fulfill. His mind was exploding with the sensation of the warmth and softness and the slight taste of grape jelly. The kiss was over before he could make sense of it all, but the joy of it lingered on. Eventually, Jack opened his eyes again. She was gone. For a fraction of a second, he thought it actually had been a dream, but he quickly realized that she had only taken a couple of steps off the blanket. Unfortunately, she was walking away again.

"Please. You can't do this to me again. Have you no heart, my lady?" asked Jack, trying to convey his desperation.

"I am not sure what you mean," was her honest response.

"What is your name? And may I call on you some time?

She was amused by how formal a young cow herder could try to be. "I am very tempted to have you go to town and describe me to everyone." Jack was very willing to do just that.

"Yet, I have had such a wonderful time here in your meadow, by your lovely stream. I suppose

I owe you that." His eyes lit up. "My name is Hannah. The name I promised you one day is Lochrann."

"Hannah Lochrann. That is beautiful and mysterious sounding. And may I…"

"You may." She continued backing away from him. Jack seemed to instinctively understand that he should stay on the blanket.

"Can you tell me where I might find you or do I have to go door to door?" She laughed one final time before turning away, tempted to have him investigate her, looking to find her home. Yet, she could not resist telling him some more, hoping it would encourage him.

"My father is the postmaster, perhaps you have already met him. My mother is a seamstress and does laundry." She took a few more steps and then added, "If I am not there, you may find me at my older sister's home. She is married to the farrier in town." Not looking back, she continued across the meadow.

"I will find you!" he called out.

"I hope so," she said gently, not wanting him to hear her say it.

Jack fell onto his back, trying to remember all of the details, all of the sensations, of his first meaningful kiss. It was a long time before he got back to his uncle's cattle.

Chapter Four

...because all life is based on it.

John opened his eyes and looked straight up into a sterile and clinical-looking ceiling. The more it came into focus the drabber it appeared. He was somewhat frozen, but not by fear. Confusion held him in place at first. Pain kept him there after that. He was lying down and could feel a sheet and blanket covering three-fourths of his body. Music was playing lightly somewhere behind him. John had heard the tune before, but could not name it. The sound was that of swing music, but this was no dance hall. The whole situation was bizarre and began to unnerve him. Where was Lana? Where was Father Rick? He tried to speak, but with the first movement of his tongue, John knew he would not be successful. There was a dryness he had never known. No hangover or physical exertion had ever made his mouth this dry. "Hhh...hhh...help me," came out as a whisper. He heard a response but it was not directed at him.

"Dr. Way. Dr. Way! He's awake, Dr. Way. The patient in bed three is awake." John heard a woman's heels walking away very quickly. The last thing he heard her say made no sense to him. "Should I go tell the reporters?" John could not hear the response to the question and had no context. It just added to his disorientation.

Somewhere to John's right a tinny speaker stopped playing music and turned to the voice of a radio announcer. "That was the sound of Arthur Tracy, playing a sweet song called 'East of the Sun (and West of the Moon).' Next up on the KDKA New Music Hour, a tune from the Broadway musical, 'Jubilee.' This is Judith Knight singing 'Begin the Beguine.'" Music, with a surprisingly sad jazz beat, began to play, but John's attention was drawn away from it.

He heard the solid step of a man's shoes approaching. "Thank you, nurse. I'll talk to him. And at this time tell no one else." John did not turn to look at the man he assumed was a doctor. Memories started to come back, stimulated by the pain he felt. The slightest movement of his head made his neck, back, and shoulder twitch in agony. A chair slid across the floor, and John felt the presence of someone to his left. A shadow came over his face, and he suddenly felt a cold sensation on his lips and tongue. The fog was still lifting. Clarity was approaching. John surmised that the doctor was holding an ice cube to his lips. He breathed in through his mouth, drawing in some water. There were only a few drops, but all things are relative. At this moment, it was the most refreshing thing that he could remember in his life.

"Th...thanks."

"Don't talk." The doctor placed a hand on John's left shoulder to establish a physical connection. It was an old belief in many who worked in the healing arts.

Some thought it superstition, but in a place like Quehanna, many still believed there was a degree of power in the touch between humans. Some had it more than others, but it was always there. "I'm Dr. Way. I'm the head surgeon here. You've been through a lot, Detective Leary." The physician tried to smile in a friendly way and say something funny. "I bet you'll think twice before coming back to coal country again." He patted John gently. The surgeon allowed John to think about what he had said for a moment, giving their connection more time to be established. "Just rest. If you are fully awake and feel strong enough, I can try to go through what's happened to you." John moved his head a little, signaling his acquiescence. "Okay. Let's start at the top." The doctor did not hesitate, seeming almost eager to discuss his work. "Your right clavicle is fractured, here at the conoid tubercle." The doctor touched John's left collarbone to illustrate what he was saying about his right side. "One piece of buckshot hit the bone directly, drove through to the corocoid process that protrudes from the scapula. It was deflected and then lodged in your medial triceps muscle right here." Again the surgeon used John's left side to help him understand what had happened on his right. "I removed that and repaired the damage. It seems that four other pieces of shot hit you in the collarbone area. You lost a large piece of the trapezius muscle, mainly in the posterior where, I believe, two pieces of shot exited." A poke of the doctor's index finger indicated exactly where the balls had exited. "I used a lot of sutures to put it back together, but you will never have full strength. Too much of the muscle was torn away."

The surgeon seemed nonchalant about it, but John began to grow highly agitated. Perhaps it was best then that the doctor quickly moved on. The detective was forced to continue listening. "The other two penetrated the right pectoral muscle just under the clavicle, here and here. They lodged in front of your right subscapular fossa, the plate, but fortunately did not hit any bone, so they did not ricochet, nor do as much damage. It was, however, tricky getting them out. Quite the challenge, but I think the surgery was much less invasive than it could have been." The doctor patted John's left shoulder and continued, asking, "Am I being too technical, Detective Leary?"

For a moment John could not decide if he should shake his head or try to speak. Neither seemed like a good option. "No," he whispered, deciding that speech was the less painful of the two. It was only a small lie. He wanted to say more, tell him that he had some training and knew some of the words he was using, but one grunt was all he could muster.

"Okay. I'm sure you realize that your arm is in a sling. You will need to keep that as steady and motionless as possible. We can't put your collarbone in a cast, so we have to immobilize it as best we can." John heard the chair slide. Though the blanket was not covering his left side and leg already, he felt the doctor push it back some more. "Now let's talk about the damage here." The doctor did not put his hands on John this time. Unconsciously, it made the detective wary. How bad was the wound if a surgeon did not want to even get close to it?

"This wound was simpler in a way. The damage was more confined, but also more extensive." The surgeon paused, realizing the statement would confuse most anyone. "Let me explain. The buckshot that hit you here did not ricochet and tear through your organs. Only one piece of shot perforated your large intestine. We operated there first to clean and close those wounds. Hopefully, we can prevent sepsis. Another shot penetrated, but upon hitting your left os coxae...I'm sorry, I mean your hip bone. Once they hit the bone they ricocheted away from your organs, and tore through skin and muscle, particularly the oblique. This is very dense muscle and might, perhaps, heal almost completely. The only problem is that some of your pelvis was shattered, particularly at the iliac crest and the anterior superior spine." Dr. Way paused for a moment and John wondered if always used such esoteric anatomical jargon with his patients.

Dr. Way took a deep breath, and John tried to focus his mind, expecting more medical terminology. At the same time, the doctor was reminding himself to keep it simple. "It was an awful mess and will be a long time in healing, but as long as we can stop any infection, you should do fine. A few other pieces of shot tore away some flesh but were not serious, relatively speaking of course. As I tried to say, the damage was intense, but not extensive in terms of the amount of your body wounded. Other than the wound to your intestine, you have damage to one shoulder and one hip bone. That's not bad for being in a gunfight with a ten gauge shotgun at close range." The doctor looked down on John, expecting that statement to elicit a response. He was disappointed. "Now then, this will take a lot of care on our part, and a lot of hard work on your part. For now, I've left the incision I used to operate on the intestine open to drain. Our nurses will monitor it around the clock." John had closed his eyes during the description, trying to be as clinical as the doctor, even though it was his flesh that had been ripped apart and his bones that had been broken. It was difficult to keep control of the anxiety growing inside him. He heard the doctor stand and sensed a shadow upon him. He opened his eyes to see a doctor that looked about his age standing over him. It did not match the image he had formed. To John, the voice seemed much older. Although the face was younger than John pictured it, the expression on it was not uplifting. Still, it was not foreboding. The look on the doctor's face only held pity for what had already been done, not what might happen. Yet the melancholy in the voice was still present. "Do you have any questions of me, Detective Leary?"

"Father Rick?" asked John quietly. The surgeon pursed his lips and shook his head.

"As you might remember, Father Rick was hit in the leg. That wound was not as severe as you might think." The doctor paused. "A good-sized man, large legs. The shot did some damage, but did not hit anything vital like the femoral artery."

John nodded his head and whispered, "Lana?"

"Oh, yes. Other than getting me for a surgeon, I would say Mrs. Hammond was the best thing for you. She alerted the authorities. Dressed your wounds and stopped the bleeding. Kept you warm. If not for her, you would have never met me."

"Where are...where you from?" John was running out of energy, yet he required more information. Something told him he knew the surgeon somehow. Yet, he could not recall ever meeting him.

"Just like you, Detective Leary, I come from the hills around Ben Nevis, although I'm a few years older. George Way, Casonville, Class of 1910."

"War," was the only word John could muster for a short time. Then he whispered, "You're a...hero."

"I don't know about that. After medical school at Penn, I was lucky enough to be given an all-expense-paid trip to France. Didn't do anything heroic. Took some shrapnel in my back when some German artillery exploded while I was outside our makeshift hospital, trying to assess some of the wounded. Right place, wrong time." The doctor looked carefully at John's expression, which was terribly pained. Quickly he realized that his self-deprecation was not that funny to John, at least not as funny as Dr. Way found it. Instead, he tried to make an actual joke. "I left the hospital and got myself wounded. Usually, it's the other way around." The doctor smiled, but it only seemed weary, not enlightening. "I'm being cynical of course, but in truth, this was lucky for you. I have a lot of experience with wounds like this. My colleagues here do not. Anyway, you're the real hero here. Newspapermen have been wanting to see you, even though you've been unconscious for days. I've kept them away for now."

"Thank..." He could not finish expressing his gratitude. The energy seemed to be gone, and he closed his eyes for a moment.

"I'll make sure the nurse gives you some more ice, or water if you can drink some. Let her know if the pain increases beyond what you can tolerate. Otherwise, your next medication will be given in about two hours. I'll be on duty for just a little longer, but I will check in on you tomorrow, Detective Leary." The doctor was finished talking with his patient, but John sensed he wanted to say more. He wanted to make more of a connection but had no idea where to go with the conversation beyond the medical. Quickly, he latched onto the first thing he could. "Enjoy the music. It's the latest addition from our new administrator." The sentence ended with a touch of disdain in his voice. "Feels some pleasant background music helps patients heal. Personally, I think it should just be quiet resting." John opened his eyes again, in time to see the doctor pat him one final time on the left shoulder and walk away.

John heard his footsteps on the wood floor growing fainter. For the first time, he looked around as much as his limited movement would allow. It appeared that he was in a hospital ward instead of a room. Although he could not see far, it did seem as though there were more beds on either side of him. The ward was quiet, other than the music playing, but John had sensitive hearing. Someone to his left was not breathing regularly. They seemed to be struggling. Further away, on his right, was a patient who seemed to be crying or weeping. John decided to listen to the music instead but heard it stop just as he changed his focus.

"And that wraps up the KDKA New Music Hour. We hope you enjoyed these songs. They are sure to be big hits here in Pittsburgh during the coming weeks. Now taking us into the next hour is a modern-day classic of our times. This is Bing Crosby with my own personal mantra, "Brother Can You Spare a Dime?" The theme song for John's generation began to play. The radio announcer spoke over the song one last time. "And remember the news will be coming up right after this." A woman's shoes approached.

"Hello, Detective Leary. My name is Rose. I'll be your nurse tonight. It's good to see you awake finally." John tried to speak but felt dizzy. His head was spinning a little, even though he was lying down. "You just rest now. I only need to check your vitals." She held his left wrist up and seemed to turn away to the left. John forced himself to think about what was happening. He did not like these feelings of helplessness and resignation. After a few seconds, he decided the nurse was looking at a clock somewhere to his left. He did not have any desire to turn his head for confirmation of his hypothesis, but he felt better just for keeping his mind focused. After a minute she put his arm down and recorded something on a clipboard. She then asked, "Detective Leary, do you think you can hold this in your mouth? I need to get your temperature, hoping there's no sign of infection." John just nodded his head slightly to indicate he could. The nurse placed the thermometer in his mouth. She moved off to the stand beside his bed. John could hear her pouring water. Time seemed to move awfully slowly, but she finally pulled the thermometer from his mouth and read it. "You're a little hot, but nothing alarming. We'll keep an eye on it, don't worry." After recording the temperature, she brought the edge of a cup to his lips. "Just a little drink. We don't want you to get dehydrated. Not too much at first though." It was even lovelier than the ice.

John felt another presence approach his bed. An older nurse stood on his right. She did not acknowledge him. "Rose, Mrs. Knepper is complaining about the pain again. She's allowed some more before her next dose..." The nurse lowered her voice to a whisper. "...but, I want you to make sure you chart everything. I think she might be getting to like the medicine a little too much." The volume of her voice rose again. "And how are you, Detective Leary. You certainly seem to be able to take the pain. Dr. Way get you all fixed up?" John could not answer her, but it was not due to the weakness he felt. The nurse named Rose was still giving him one more, small sip of water. Then she walked away to take care of Mrs. Knepper.

John nodded and then said in an almost inaudible voice, "He's a hero. He's...He's from my...hometown."

The second nurse did not respond with any discreetness. "Hero," she said dismissively. "More like a drunk if you ask me."

"What?" asked John. There was indignation in his voice, but it was so low the nurse did not notice.

"Let's just say you're lucky you caught him on a good day." There was no chance for John to respond. As the nurse began to walk away, for all to hear, she boldly proclaimed, "That man keeps going the way he is, he'll die young. I swear he will. Cirrhosis going to..." John could hear no more as she passed through the swinging doors to his right.

John knew better than to listen to workplace gossip, but his mind was not focused. It felt as though a fog had descended on him again. His sight was not blurred, but his mind's eye was. Disappointment was the overwhelming feeling growing in him. It was not because someone, even a heroic veteran of the war, had succumbed to the demon, alcohol. That was not a rare occurrence. John knew the reason he felt distraught to hear this was the fact that his father had held the good doctor in such high esteem. When John was a teenager, his father had told him the whole story about George Way saving soldiers on the Western Front in France. He made John read all the articles about him. He was a hometown boy made good. Now, he was back in his hometown. Was he any better off than Lana, who had never left?

John needed to stop thinking about it. His ear caught the change in sound from the speaker. The music had died away and a man was reading the news. His subconscious had already started listening to it, drawn to its familiarity. "A disturbing story comes out of Quehanna County in the central part of the state. Six days ago, on October thirty-first, near the small town of Ben Nevis, a farmer, apparently enraged over alleged acts of Halloween vandalism, shot and killed two young teenagers. According to reports, a state police officer, named John Leary, responding to the incident and killed the man, but was severely wounded himself. Leary is a detective with the Pennsylvania State Police and is assigned to the Butler barracks. However, he is originally from Ben Nevis, and is still hospitalized in Quehanna Memorial Hospital near there. In addition, Monsignor Richard Hooker, attending to the dying children, was also wounded and later died of an apparent heart attack. State police report that further investigation of the shooting is pending, but that no arrests are likely. The farmer, one Herman Rotz, apparently acted..."

At first John was confused, having never heard something about himself on a news report. Even though he had been involved in several, high-profile cases, he did not own a radio and had never heard a case described on the air. His wife always enjoyed live music more. They loved to go dancing, and when she died, so had the music. Despite Pittsburgh having the very first radio station in the country, John never bought one and rarely listened to broadcasts when given the chance. About halfway through the news report, John recognized what the announcer was saying, but he still could not believe it. Why had Dr. Way lied to him? No. John quickly realized that he had not lied. Why had he not told him the full truth? Where was he? What the hell was going on? "Waaaaayyyyy!" The violence of his eruption lifted him off the pillows slightly. The movement hurt as much as the buckshot had. John's body collapsed back into the mattress. His body was suddenly wracked with spasms, but his anger would not subside. No one answered. John was not even sure he had made a loud enough sound, but the pain was too intense for him to try again. He had known enough pain in his life. In fact, it had become his life. The time had come to move past it. "Nuuurrrssse!" John felt stitches tear open as his chest sunk in again. He began to thrash, trying to sit up. He reached a high watermark of getting his good elbow under his side and propping himself up. Once more he attempted to scream for the nurse, but a ripping pain running down his throat caught him off guard and he swallowed the word.

It did not matter because the older nurse was rushing into the ward, indignant that a patient was disturbing everyone's rest. "What is going on in here?" she called out. John watched her approach while he tried to summon some saliva to soothe his sore throat. "Detective Leary! You cannot go on shouting like that!" Her voice screeched. The irony fled before her, never allowing the nurse to grasp it. "You are disturbing other patients and interfering with their..." She was close enough now for John to unleash his fury. There was no way for him to be as loud as her, but John knew how to talk softly and get his message across.

His eyes locked onto hers and would not let go. The right side of his upper lip twitched slightly, arching into a growling sneer for just a moment. The adrenaline was flowing in his veins and his eyes blazed with righteousness. John's anger was boiling over. "Do you think I give a damn?" His throat felt like it was bleeding, but John pushed on. "I want to see Dr. Way now! And he better have one hell of an explanation for lying to me." John knew it was not technically a lie, but he still felt a betrayal of trust. "Now unless you want to see how fast I can fight my way free on one leg, you turn your ass around and go find me the doctor." The nurse's mouth hung open. No patient had ever spoken to her like that. She had always overpowered people simply with her attitude, but this detective was not a normal patient. There was a look of righteous fury in his eyes that burned white-hot, even though they had been closed for almost a week. The determination that showed in his gaze informed her immediately that come hell or high water, he would get answers.

She responded with shock and histrionics. "Rose! Rose! Help me. Help me, Rose! The detective's..." The rest was muffled as the doors to the ward swung back shut. Trying to only move his eyes and not his head, John looked around a few times, listening to the sounds of the ward returning to its normal ways of meek sadness, silent fear, and the tick-tock of death waiting. The radio speakers were still playing softly. The patient who was struggling to breathe earlier was now coughing. The woman, a few beds away, was crying harder. Briefly, John wondered if it was the amount or type of pain that made her weep so demonstratively. Was it agony or angst? She was in the hospital, but it sounded like the latter, as if she needed a different type of facility. Then his own wounds overwhelmed him as most of the adrenaline slipped away. His elbow slid out, and he collapsed back into the bed. With his eyes closed, John tried to empty his mind, but could not make the images disappear.

In rapid-fire, his brain began jumping between Lana's face coming out from the shadows, Father

Rick's bear hug engulfing him, eggs running over Mark's face, the blank stare of Mrs. Bennett, the sinister grin on a child's face, the bodies on the road, and the pure hatred of Mr. Rotz's final act. He could not picture it, but the last thing he heard was the old farmer's horrified confession. The last thing he saw was his parents. They were saying goodbye to Angela as John waited at the driver's side of their car. It was a Sunday night and John and his wife were heading back to Butler. It was a memory that had come to him often after they had died, for it was the last time he had seen them. Yet, this time they were not saying goodbye. He could not hear what they were saying, but he knew it instinctively. All of them were asking why John could not save them, even Rotz asked. The images faded away, and then, strangely enough, a picture of Dr. Way came to his mind. He asked John the same question as the others.

"Why? Why couldn't you save me?"

Then just as quickly as the hallucination had come over him, the accusatory song in his mind was suddenly replaced by a new voice in the ward. At first, John thought it was the radio, for it was a man singing, but it grew louder, and he knew someone was approaching his bed. There was a roughness to the voice, but at the same time, it was smoothed over by the sadness of the song. As he approached, he sang about his being buried by the roadside, so that his soul, or his evil spirit could catch a ride. Was that it? His soul needed catch a ride to its final destination. With those words, a chill came over John, and he knew something was wrong. Something in the hospital had been terribly changed. A darkness had fallen. The light of this world was slipping away from him. John opened his eyes to see not a doctor or nurse, but a young, Black man, pushing a wooden wheelchair. In the wheelchair sat a guitar. The sight so perplexed him that John did not speak, even though a thousand questions rushed into his mind. "Don't want to be doin' that now, Mr. Leary. You gone an done tore open some stitches there. I see the blood."

John knew that this man was no doctor. Quehanna, he was certain, was not progressive enough to have a Negro as a doctor. Unless they had become much more enlightened since John had left, the young man was not a member of the medical staff. He was clearly not an orderly or custodian either. He was dressed in a brown suit with a fedora. Yet, that did not even register in John's mind. A sudden flash of memory came over him, but he could not see anything. It was simply a feeling deep in his core. He wanted to communicate but was having difficulty. He knew he had strained his throat by shouting. In addition, he felt weak and nauseous. Still, he managed,

"Have we met?"

"Oh yes, Mr. Leary," affirmed the young man.

"Where did...where? Forgive me..." John was having trouble forming the words.

The man smiled in the friendliest of responses. "We met a long time from here, but I'm glad to be back. It's always good to come home to the times you know. The buildings, the vehicles, the music, it all makes more sense to me right now."

John could not follow what he was saying, but he saw the movement of his hands. Something tickled his brain and told him to be wary of the man's hands. He watched him take the guitar out of the chair, lovingly running his right hand across the strap. Then the man slung the instrument over his left shoulder. For a moment, John thought he was going to play a song, but he would not. In a lightning-fast spin, the guitar was moved to his back. John could see the bottom of it, now raised above his shoulder, and the neck sticking out from behind his hip. The man walked easily a few steps, pushing the wheelchair forward. He stopped at the head of John's bed and spun the chair around so that it was now pointed in the direction it had come.

The pain, fatigue, and nausea faded away. All John felt now was a growing sense of anxiety. This was all wrong. Everything was wrong. "There are some more tests that we have to do, Mr. Leary. Yes, sir. More tests to come."

"What?" was all John could muster for a few ticks of the clock on the far wall to his left, which John could suddenly hear over all the noises in the ward. The man stepped closer. His sharply pleated pants leg pushed into the pillow propping up John's damaged arm. "You people know what's wrong with me," he cried. For the first time since his wife's passing, John felt helpless. Suddenly, he knew what made the woman in the bed across the aisle weep. "I've been shot."

"Oh, that ain't all that's wrong." The man's hands were quickly thrust under John's body. In one fluid movement, he was picked up. Now it was John's turn to be in awe. The man was not big enough to throw someone John's size around like this. How could this be happening? He stepped back and deposited John's body into the wheelchair with no regard for the pain it caused. And it did cause pain, terrible, monstrous pain. "Aaaaahhhhh!" cried John. The burning and ripped throat was still there, but John felt none of that compared to the shredding of the wound to his intestines. "Aww, Judas priest. What the hell?" They were meant to be expletives, but John's tired voice could manage only a few decibels. The burning and pinching of his hip spread out through his entire body. Stitches in his shoulder came loose completely, sending sharp bolts up his neck, paralyzing the right side of his face. Fresh blood began to flow from his wounds, washing away the dark, dry, congealed blood around them. John shook his head, unable to make the pain dissipate. A childlike "Help!" escaped from his mouth, but it was all he could generate. The circuitry of his brain was being overwhelmed. His vision went black and he almost lost consciousness. The man in the brown suit remained steadfast and calm.

"Well, Mr. Leary, I am afraid it is time for your next appointment. I'd love to sit and listen to music with you, maybe chat a little, but we've got to be going."

"Hey! What are you doing with him?" the coughing man barked.

The man in the brown suit turned and took the full measure of the patient. "You just never mind what I'm doing. Less you want to be next." The man saw a look in his eyes that told him it was no idle threat. He shut his mouth and eyes at the same time and pulled the sheet and blanket a little higher. The man tipped his fedora to the patient and said, "Dr. Way and Nurse Rose will be right back as soon as they're done having a drink and a little more down in the janitor's closet." Then he turned back around and pushed John, whose eyes were starting to spasm, toward the exit. With a disorienting abruptness, the man stopped pushing the chair. At a pace that revealed his mistake, he went back to John's bed and poured a full glass of ice water. As he came back to the chair, he lowered the ice water over John's right shoulder and placed it on his hand. "Now, you hold on to this Mr. Leary, case you get thirsty there. The heat of the moment can be overwhelming, so I hear," Delirium was overtaking John. Without a thought, he grasped the cool, wet glass.

A few seconds later they burst through the swinging doors and John was faced with the terrible planning of the hospital. All that lay in front of him was a set of cold, forbidding stairs. There were too many steps for him to count in the brief amount of time he was given. The brim of the man's fedora pushed against John's fevered brow and suddenly sweat-soaked hair. He whispered in John's ear, "If people like you had won, you'd have kept people like me down. Kept me as a slave." He reached over John's shoulder and removed the glass of ice water from his hand. As if casting a spell, he waved his hand over the water and then dipped his fingers into it, stirring the shards of ice. Then he sprinkled drops onto John's head. Finally, he touched his moistened fingers to John's lips. With a slow deliberation, he carefully set the water down on the concrete. Then he returned to whispering to the wounded detective. The pain had driven John to paralysis and he simply listened helplessly. "How am I gonna make my music when you got me pickin' cotton all day?" It was on the "d" of the last word that he gave the wheelchair a tremendous thrust.

The chair flew over the first three steps, but then hit the fourth and overturned, sending

John flying forward. He first hit the stairs with his good shoulder, which separated in the next instant. John did not even feel it. There was no time. His body flipped over and his good hip smashed into the right angle of a step, breaking the pelvis in two places. Somehow John's head avoided making more than a scraping connection with stairs, but his momentum was too much to hold him at one revolution. The inertia of his body could not be stopped without a lot of force. He was shot forward toward the landing where the stairs switched direction. A cold, gray, cement-block wall hurtled toward him. John tried to get his hands up in time, but with all of his injuries and a sling, it was not to be. His forehead and left eye socket hit the bricks first. It produced a "thud!" that always makes people grimace, yet at the top of the stairs, the young man watched impassively. John's body seemed to hold in mid-air for the tiniest of moments and then the wheelchair caught up with him. It was only a grazing blow, but the wood and steel chair was heavy, and its impact spun his body around. He collapsed on the landing in a position on his side, looking up. Now he blankly gazed back up the stairwell. The image was blurred and fading quickly. He could see a fuzzy image of the man kneeling down to pick something up. The next thing he sensed was the hearing of glass smashing against the wall he himself had just hit, and the feeling of shock as water, ice, and glass hit his body in various spots. To the man who had done this, he did protest the action. Yet, all John could say was, "This isn't right. I don't belong here." Then the world disappeared into the darkness.

Chapter Five

...because we were all wounded thus.

"I'm tired, Jacks. Could you go check on Ellie? See what she wants."

"Sure." Jackson leaned over and gave the back of her head a kiss. "Sure, Lenore." She did not like it when he rhymed her name like that. A hand swatted at him playfully, but even in the dark he was able to dodge it. Jackson got up from the bed and began to leave the room. He momentarily stopped and pondered whether he needed to put on his pants. Then he shook his head, realizing it didn't matter if he walked into Ellie's room in his long johns. He was still shaking his head as he left the room. It was a short distance to the child's bedroom. He quickly walked over to the girl's small bed, knelt down beside her, and stroked her hair.

"Mr. Jacks? Is that you?"

"It is. I'm here, Miss Electa." He was the only one who used her given name. Everyone else called her Ellie or Elle. She called him Mr. Jacks and in return, he called her Miss Electa. Though she was a young child, only seven years old, Jackson tried to speak to her like an older girl. At times, it seemed like everyone else wanted to baby or coddle her. He could not know for certain, but he thought little Ellie had accepted him because of his faith that she could handle more. "Your mother's sleeping. Can I help?"

"No. Well. I guess so. Momma told me to tell her the next time my friend came." This was the first time Jackson had heard about Ellie's friend.

"There was someone in your room, sweetie?"

"Yes. No. I guess it was just a dream. That's what Momma says it is." Jackson had never thought about it before, but suddenly he had an intense interest. He was curious about what Ellie's dreams were like. Did they have color? Would she know what things were? How was her mind generating them? Before he asked her a question, he asked himself an age-old one. What are dreams?

"Tell me, Miss Electa. What did you dream about?"

"My friend. She came to see me again. She's so pretty. I like her."

"What were you and your friend doing?" Jackson found this fascinating.

"It was great, Mr. Jacks. We were in this large meadow. It was a field of flowers. We kept chasing butterflies all over the..." The little girl paused. Jackson thought about what she described. He could see that her dreams were real, but they probably were not like his. Ellie had experienced flowers and meadows, and even butterflies, in her own way. "I almost forgot Mr. Jacks."

"What? What did you forget?"

"My friend told me to tell you something." Ellie was teasing him a little.

"Okay, Miss Electa. I'll play along. What did your friend say to tell me?"

"Well, she didn't say, 'Tell Mr. Jacks,' but I'm pretty sure she meant you."

"All right, I'm all ears." He reached out and tickled her ears, and Ellie giggled.

"She said..." The little girl paused, trying to elicit another response from Jackson, but he was not picking up on the cue. "She said, 'The firewood and the powder will not save them, but the door will save you." Jackson was waiting for more, but that was all Ellie gave him. Silence came over the room as Jackson tried to figure out the message.

He was never one for riddles. "Miss Electa? Can you tell me what that means?"

"I don't know. She just told me to tell you. Made me say it back to her a couple of times." In the dim light, Jackson could see a look of worry on her face, as if she was anxious to get it just right.

"Is this a place out in the barn?"

"I don't know."

"Did she say anything else?" The little girl looked down at her covers. She fidgeted for a few seconds. "Miss Electa, was there more?"

"She told me something about her friend, Elizabeth, but I can't remember." The little girl paused and then added an unnecessary apology, "I'm sorry, Mr. Jacks."

"Oh, it's just fine, honey." He rubbed her back. "You know why?" She shook her head to indicate that she did not. "Cause I don't know what it means any way." A smile came over her face. Jackson smiled too, but he was still curious. "What's your friend's name, Sweetie?"

"She doesn't have a name, Mr. Jacks. She's just my friend. We play together. She's really pretty...but sometimes she's sad. One time she told me she never had any children of her own." Ellie smiled. There was little light in the room, but Jackson could see the expression. It confused him.

"Sweetie, why are you smiling?"

"Not tonight, but one time she told me that if she had had a girl she would've wanted them to be just like me." Jackson now smiled, but it was imbued with sadness, and he was glad that Ellie could not see that.

"I know exactly what your friend means. Now you need to get some sleep. I'll tell your momma that your friend was here. She'll talk to you in the morning. Miss Electa, are you going to be all right?"

"Yes, Mr. Jacks. I'll be fine."

"And if you get any more messages for me, you'll let me know?" Jackson ran his hand over her hair and then bent down and kissed her on the forehead. She smiled and shook her head, but did not say anymore. He turned away and walked back to the room he often shared with Lenore. He ducked his head under the frame of the door and wondered how Lenore's husband could have been such a poor carpenter. The farm was still well-run in terms of the crops and the livestock, but it seemed that nothing was square and no size was standard. Perhaps it did not matter to other folks, but Jackson knew that was one of the reasons he had bought the adjacent farm. Its house, barn, and corn cribs were very well constructed. Even the outhouse was nice and sturdy. In addition, the house sat on a little rise that overlooked the neighboring farms, some of the prettiest country in all of Pennsylvania. The house rested amongst an apple orchard, one that still produced sweet, delicious fruit. Yes, he had made wise use of the money he had come into. He thought of his home some more as he lied down beside Lenore. She had turned over and taken the blankets away, but that did not bother him. After a cold streak had brought October to an end, the first day of November had been surprisingly warm. Jackson stared at the rough-hewn ceiling above him and decided he would ask Lenore to move up to his house. It would be the third or fourth time he had asked, for he wanted to make a home with her and Ellie, not just keep coming over like a guest. He had known them for over a year now. Something special had developed between them. Yet, this house belonged to another man, one that was now gone. She would tell him she understood, and maybe someday she would move up the hill, but not until Ellie was a good bit older. This had been her home since she was born. She knew where everything was and could get around very easily. And that would end the conversation. Jackson would not go against Lenore's desire to protect Ellie, but it did not sit well with him.

For close to a hour he was on his back, wanting to go to sleep, but his mind would not stop working. This was not normal for Jackson. Anytime someone asked him what he was thinking about, he would respond as most men did, "Nothing." The vast majority of the time he was being truthful. Now myriad thoughts danced in Jackson's head, which actually bothered him. He considered himself a simple man, just happy to have a good day's work and a hot meal. Yet, for the past two days something had been bothering him, something he could not identify. Often, he had found himself looking for something, yet not knowing what he was searching for. A lot of details were observed, most of them meaningless. There was no clarity and nothing was concrete. It seemed like something was moving at the edge of his vision, but when he turned to look, whatever it had been had vanished. The presence was gone.

At this moment, he was noticing every little jab from the mattress. A different revelation came to him as well. His feet were cold. He tried to slide his feet under the covers that Lenore was holding tightly, but was only partially successful. Usually, he loved lying in Lenore's bed. It was not the bed of a wealthy socialite, but it was so much better than anything Jackson had ever known. He had gone from a wood slat with some blankets at his childhood home in Virginia to sleeping on the ground or a rough cot in the army. Lenore's bed had felt so warm and welcoming on the first night they had been together that Jackson asked her where he could purchase one like it for his own home. Lenore had seductively told him that if he played his cards right, he wouldn't need to purchase one. Thinking of that allowed his mind to relax some.

Yet, once he felt comfortable in the bed, he heard every noise from outside and every creak of the farmhouse on the inside. The wind seemed to be picking up. No matter how empty he let his thoughts become, he could not let the world go. He decided he was simply looking for irritating things, so he focused his mind on the words Ellie had said, the message from her dream. What could they mean? Why would Ellie tell him that? If she had made it up, what was she trying to say to him? Over and over, he repeated them in his mind. Slowly, his insomnia wore down, and he finally gave in. Jackson's eyelids closed and unconsciousness rolled over him.

It did not last the night though. He woke with a start and quickly looked around. No shadows danced, for Lenore's bedroom did not have a window. No sounds spooked him. He listened for the wind, but there was none. Yet, something was amiss. A chill came over him and he thought about pulling the covers from Lenore. Instead, he got up from the bed. Once again, he walked to Ellie's room. She was fine, wrapped in her blankets almost exactly like her mother. Jackson watched her body rise and fall a few times in the dim moonlight coming through the window in Ellie's room. Jackson was proud of that window. He had suggested it to Lenore and they had saved some money for it. Jackson had put it in a few months ago. It looked out toward the barn that was behind the house, but that was not why he wanted to frame it up and install it. It looked beyond the barn to the southeast. In the morning when the sun rose, the room was filled with light. Ellie was able to experience a little of that, if mainly by the feel of the sunshine on her face. The child had told Jackson that she always loved waking up to a "sunshiney" day. The man smiled at that memory, but only briefly. Something still ached in his brain. There was a slight dread in his nerves since waking. He thought of going over to the window and turning to the southwest. If you looked carefully you could see his house sitting on the low rise at the base of the ridge. Then, just as quickly, he decided against it.

"No, Miss Electa," he said to the sleeping child. "It's been over five years. I'm done looking over my shoulder." Jackson stepped back from her doorway and walked on toward the tiny washroom at the end of the second floor. There, on a small table were two pitchers. One was for washing and had a large bowl in front of it. A smaller pitcher was to the right. Lenore left it, and a small cup, in the exact same spot so that Ellie could get a drink in the night if she needed it. Jackson had taken to leaving the metal cup he drank coffee from behind the pitcher in case he also needed a drink. The pain of a dry, scratchy throat pushed him toward the water. The simple touch of the cool metal against his lips felt very soothing, yet it was the water that brought him peace. Jackson poured a little more into his cup and then drank it down. In the darkness, he looked at the cup, barely able to see its dull, corroded metal. He thought about pouring another cup and drinking it, but he wanted to make sure there was still some for Ellie. And he certainly did not feel like going out to the pump. Still, he was tempted. Since yesterday, Jackson had felt terribly dehydrated. He could not explain his sudden thirst and hoped he was not getting sick. The harvest was done, but his farm, and Lenore's, had to be prepared for winter. A farmer could not afford to miss a day of work. For a brief moment, Jackson pictured himself sick and in bed. He imagined Lenore caring for him. The image he dreamed up had him with a fever, but that was not what gathered his focus. It was his bed. "My bed," he said to no one, but in those words he realized the current arrangement was silly. It needed to change.

Back to Lenore's room he walked with a renewed purpose. The floor creaked as he stepped through the doorway and closed the door behind him. He knew the floorboard was loose and usually tried to step over it in the night to not wake Lenore. This time he wanted it to disturb her. It did not. She was sleeping soundly as he came to the side of the bed. There was very little light in the room. Only some reflected moonlight from the hallway illuminated her enough for Jackson to see the outline of Lenore's body. He reached out to stroke his hand through her hair. Instead, his hand hit her in the forehead. Jackson felt foolish but tried to quickly move to his target, hoping her unconsciousness would work in his favor. She woke slowly, and only noticed him running his fingers through her hair.

Jackson turned away from her and picked up his pants from the floor. He reached into a pocket and pulled a box of lucifers from it. Lenore would never allow it in her home, but Jackson learned to appreciate a good cigar when he was in the army, and many times a bad cigar as well. He tried to enjoy one whenever he could, but this match was meant for something else. He struck the match, watched the red tip come to life, and then lit the candle sitting on the nightstand.

"Why are you lighting that?" asked Lenore, shielding her eyes for a moment. She yawned deeply.

"I want...I need to see your face." Jackson did not have an elaborate plan. He simply turned to her and asked, "Lenore, will you marry me?"

Lenore looked at him softly. She was not smiling. Nor were there any tears welling up in her eyes. She was making it hard for Jackson to get a read on her emotions. There was a glow to her face that did not come from the candle. She seemed content to Jackson, but he was not certain. He realized that it might be the fact that she was not awake yet. She took a deep breath, but still did not respond. Finally, she smiled. Softly Lenore said to him. "Jacks, I love you. But I can't..." She paused, and Jackson's heart sank. They had talked several times about Lenore and Ellie moving up to his place, but he had never actually asked her to marry him. Now he had taken that leap, and it seemed a chasm was about to open up before him. He wanted to say something, anything that might save the moment. Silently he cursed himself for being slow-witted. There was nothing he could think of to change the fact that she was going to turn him down. Only a moment had passed, but the disappointment was already making his stomach feel like he had been kicked in the groin. After an agonizing few seconds she finished her thought. "I can't answer before you tell me something." A rush of relief flooded into his head and chest. Jackson could breathe a little easier.

"What do you want to know?" he asked almost giddily. The simple fact that she had not turned him down was enlightening. He imagined how amazing it would feel if she had responded positively. His joy was not long-lived.

"I have known you for over a year. We've become about as close as two people can in that time. You are so dear to me, and to Ellie. Yet, I've known since the beginning that there are things you cannot share with me. Some of it is the war. I reckon some of it came after the war." He looked at her with a volatile mix of anxiety and curiosity. She dismissed it quickly.

"You talk in your sleep sometimes."

They stared at each other for a moment and then, in flash of emotion, Jackson remembered how good she made him feel, how secure he felt with her, and once more he decided that Lenore could be trusted. "You don't really want to know that stuff."

"It's not that I want to know, Jacks. I want to help you stop dreaming about it. I want you to let it go. But, that's not what holds me back. I love you, but I don't have to marry. Ellie and me have been on our own for a few years now. What I need to know is that you love me."

"I do. I haven't shied away from telling you that."

"That's true. Still..." She did not want to say what had been bothering her. She did not want to push the issue, because she feared that would not be all she pushed away. "All I know...and you know it too...there's something that stands between us. It's always been there."

A terrible silence was what grew between them in that moment. It even seemed to be overwhelming the light of the candle, which suddenly flickered as if a breeze had blown through the room. Neither of them felt anything though. Finally, Jackson laughed a little and shook his head nervously. "Lenore, I'm sorry, I just don't know what you're talking about at

all." Despite his best effort to seem playful, a sadness came to his eyes.

Immediately she answered, "It's your wife, Jacks." He could hear the exasperation in her voice. "You can't talk about your wife. You won't even say her name. I'm sorry. Please understand. I'm not asking you to forget her. I know a part of your heart will always belong to her. No one can understand that more than me. But, before I answer you, I have to be sure you can move on, that you can be here in the present with me and Ellie."

"I'm not following you. What is it you want, Lenore? I don't...I don't know..." He rubbed his hands together, diverted his eyes down, and pursed his lips. Jackson could feel the stomach acid rising up in his throat. It was an involuntary response that he could not seem to stop.

"That's it. I want to know. I just want to know about her, about the two of you. I just need to know that you've faced up to her death, and can move on." Silence filled the room again. Jackson got up and walked to the other side of the bed. He sat down at the same time Lenore sat up.

He was going to say something just to end the silence. Then he saw her lips begin to part and he held his tongue, waiting for something that might help him make a decision. He had never thought she would go to this place, a place he never wanted to visit again. She shifted behind him, put her arms around his shoulders, and kissed the back of his neck. She squeezed him gently and then sat back on the bed. "Let me tell you about Mahlon."

"You have," he reminded her.

"I know, but let me show what I need from you."

"You need honesty. I ain't the brightest, but I can see that, Lenore."

"Just hush, Jacks. Or aren't you serious?" He was hurt by her tone as much as her words, but chose not to address it.

"Sorry. Go ahead."

She did not like the tone of his voice either, but Lenore understood how difficult this was. "I know I've told you some things, so I won't bore you with all the details, but it's important to me that you know what I had with Mahlon, so that you and I can go forward." Jackson sensed there was something positive in that statement. There was a promise of possibility. It made him turn around to face her. He leaned in and their eyes met in the dim light of the candle. Lenore took a short breath and began.

"Mahlon came to Gettysburg when he was twelve. His father came to teach at the college. He had been at the college's medical school in Philadelphia, but he wanted to move his family away from the city. I got to know Mahlon and his sister at school that fall. I was just ten at the time. We were friends. I was more friends with his sister than him. After I turned twelve my parents took me out of school. No need for a girl to go further. Mahlon kept going of course. He was so smart, smarter than our teacher, to be sure. After I got taken out of school, I only saw Mahlon at the Meeting. His family had long been part of the Friends back in Philadelphia. Course we couldn't talk much at the Meeting, but our families sometimes came together for meals. When I was sixteen…" Lenore's voice trailed off. She seemed to be momentarily lost in the memories. Whether good or bad there can be sadness in a memory simply because it is lost to the past and will never come again.

"That's when we started to court. Unfortunately, for me, Mahlon went back to Philadelphia not long after that." Lenore's brow furrowed slightly. Jackson could see a look of consternation come over her briefly, but he was not sure what dismayed her. "We had talked about him going to college, but I always thought he would just go where his dad worked." She sighed deeply, almost wistfully. "Well, life doesn't always go the way you plan. His dad made him go to the place he went to. University of Pennsylvania. Philadelphia. Might as well have sent him to England. I don't think I realized at first how he would be gone for so long. His life was there. Mine was here. And I missed him terribly. Then one day after Meeting, his sister, Miriam, shows me a letter. Mahlon had asked about me. Said he was really busy, but desperately missed me. I practically floated home. It took a while, but I finally got up the courage to write him a letter." Lenore hesitated. She was a bit embarrassed, but decided the whole point of this was to be honest. "Actually, the first few times, I had Miriam write them. I hadn't done much writing since leaving school."

She thought about where she was headed with her story and decided to shorten it. What she wanted was Jackson's story. "Mahlon didn't write back for a while, but I'll always remember the day my mother handed me a letter from him. I actually couldn't open it for a day. If I opened it, then the anticipation of what it held would be over. Finally, I couldn't take it any longer. You'd probably think it mundane, but that letter was poetry to me. Every day, I read it over and over. As soon as I could, I asked Miriam to help me write another one. By the time Mahlon came home that first summer, we were as close as anyone could be, having not actually seen each other. I seriously fell in love with him that summer, but in truth, I had first fallen in love with his words throughout the year. The final thing happened at the next Meeting.

"It was that final connection. Might sound silly, but it took our feelings...well it made it all grown up so to speak. He...he helped me find my... You see, Jacks, I had gone to Meetings for worship my whole life. I had sat in silence and I had listened quietly when one of the members was moved to speak. But me...I never felt the connection. I was never compelled to say anything. Not cause I was too young, or I was afraid. I just never felt anything. Mahlon was so good teaching me to listen, to really listen. He helped me find my inward light. That light helped connect me, and in a way it connected me even more to Mahlon. I knew then that we were truly meant to be together.

"I knew I would spend the rest of my life with him. We made plans to marry. As I told you before, I was shocked that his parents accepted me, but they did. We married in June before his senior year. I was pregnant with Ellie by August. We decided I should stay with my parents instead of going to Philadelphia. Mahlon graduated in the spring of '62." She thought about that for a moment. "And we were happy."

Lenore's eyes glowed in the soft candlelight. Jackson marveled at their beauty, but quickly recognized a renewed sadness growing in them. A small frown came over his face, disappointed in himself because he did not know how to take her sadness away. Lenore made eye contact again and then said, "It didn't last." A thought came to Jackson, and he wondered why he had never questioned it before.

"Why did Mahlon go to war? He was a Quake..." Jackson, as he had numerous times before, had almost forgotten that Lenore did not like the common name for her denomination. "...he was a member of your Society."

Lenore shook her head, but did not look at Jackson anymore. "The unhappiness wasn't just from Mahlon joining the army." Her reply made Jackson think she was ignoring his question. "It was because we were rejected. It wasn't by the Meeting. They didn't want any controversy, and there were other members that joined up. But, his family wanted nothing to do with us after he went to war. They just couldn't accept that he would fight. They were so against war that his father wouldn't even accept any of the members who had paid for a substitute. He said it was still supporting the evil of war. Thankfully, Pennsylvania allowed for conscientious objectors. That's what kept Mahlon out of it the first two years."

"So, why did he do it?"

"I told you about our involvement in smuggling runaways out of Maryland."

"Yes," answered Jackson with a bluntness that indicated his discomfort with the idea.

She continued on. "When Mahlon would come home from school, he would work with the local people doing this, going down into Maryland and northern Virginia, guiding them. My family would hide them till we could move them on up North. I think cause the battle here was so big that people forget we helped a number of escaped slaves before the war even started. I've never known anyone braver than those slaves...those men and women. What they went through...was unbelievable." Although Jackson had never owned a slave, and no one in his family had either, the uncomfortable feeling he had in the pit of his stomach kept growing.

"So, if you all were abo...abo...you wanted to free slaves, why did they think fighting against us was wrong?" Jackson silently reminded himself to stop saying "us" in front of Lenore.

"Well, Mahlon did too at first. It's what we believe. It's fundamental to our faith. But, you see, things had started falling apart with his family. Despite his training, he didn't follow his father into medicine, and that...ohhh my. That made his father so angry. Instead of doctoring, he got a job as a druggist with the pharmacy in Gettysburg. Old Sam Forney really liked Mahlon. I think he wanted him to take over the pharmacy once he was done. Mr. Forney just retired as a druggist last year." Lenore stopped for a few seconds, thinking about the What If? scenarios that might have been her life. Then just as quickly she put them away in the backrooms of her mind. "We lived with my parents, saving up money. Then we bought this small farm. It was in terrible shape. Mahlon had to basically rebuild this house. He did such a great job. Can you believe he did all this and never had anyone teach him any carpentry or masonry or anything?"

Lenore looked up at Jackson, who appeared dumb-founded. He made it work for him. He raised his eyebrows even further, shook his head, and said, "That's astounding."

"I know. And he had to work the farm as well. And he was still a druggist. The farm was not going to earn enough on its own those first couple of years." Lenore paused, realizing that even though it was probably unintentional, Jackson was distracting her from reaching the end of the story. She had started this in order for him to tell his own. "But, after the battle here...you see Mahlon, with his medical training, he was asked to help with all the wounded. And that's what pushed him over the edge. There was no convincing him otherwise. One night he asked me, 'If slavery was so evil, why was he letting other men fight and die to abolish it. Just couldn't live with that question anymore...I guess. He grew more and more miserable until he finally joined up. And even though he wasn't working as a doctor, I thought he might be used to treat the wounded. Instead, he went into the infantry. They actually made him an officer because of his college degree. Some folks thought it was also because of his father's political connections in Harrisburg and back in Philadelphia. His dad would never admit it, because officially he wanted nothing to do with us, but some people told me he arranged for him to be a lieutenant." She stopped talking at that point, staring at the blanket with a blank gaze, letting the sadness wash over her.

Jackson let it go for a few moments before intervening. "You don't have to tell me anymore. I know that Mahlon died at Cold Harbor."

"The last battle you were in," whispered Lenore.

"Fate," was all he could answer.

"Probably silly to some...but, it's hard for me to think otherwise."

Myriad thoughts filled both their heads. Questions flowed through their minds like wind through a tunnel. Some of it was a cold wind that they both tried to shake off. Silence overcame them. Then they heard the real wind blowing outside. The house creaked some, still no one spoke. Jackson suddenly felt tired and wished they could just go to sleep. He should have asked her at breakfast. He should have made her breakfast and then asked her. He should have gotten Ellie up early, had her help make breakfast, and then asked Lenore to marry him. Damn it!

Why had he not thought this through?

"I lost everything in that battle. At least that's what I first thought. My mother came and lived with us, helped with Ellie. I wasn't worth much." Tears were filling her eyes. They glistened in the light of the candle, but none spilled out. "The inward light held in my heart was gone. I hadn't turned against God, but I had lost the light within me, and everything before my eyes was gloomy. You know it was like there was a large tree over my world and everything was in the shade, everything was just a little darker, all the time."

Jackson finally felt a connection to the story she was telling. Apart from leaving school at a young age, all of it had seemed so foreign to him. Wiping her eyes, Lenore was somewhat relieved to hear him say, "I've stood in that shadow."

And with that, and no more prodding, he began to tell his own story. "My wife's name is...was...Anna. It was Annabel. I knew her since we were young, just kids. Like you and Mahlon, but a good bit younger. You met Mahlon when you was ten. Annabel, she moved away to Kentucky when we was about ten." Jackson tried to recall some facts, but not many came to him. "Something killed her mother." It sounded blunt, but he could not remember anything more. "Her daddy couldn't or wouldn't take care of her. Sent her back to live with her grandparents on their farm next to ours. She was my friend when she left, my best friend. She was so much more when she came back five years later. I almost didn't recognize her." Jackson stopped for a moment. Lenore thought he was taking a moment to privately remember his wife. Instead, he was debating in his mind whether to say what he felt. It took a few seconds, but he finally decided that Lenore had been very open in describing her feelings for Mahlon. "My God," he blurted out, "she was beautiful."

Despite having listened to her story, Jackson was still unsure how much detail Lenore expected. "By the time I was seventeen I'd been working a few years for some of the bigger farms. I was ready to buy a small plot of land. Purchased a few acres from the McClure family. Pa gave me a couple acres and that was more than he should've. I was ready to have a family too. Didn't have anything beyond that land to offer...to bring to a marriage with...with Annabel. All I could give her when I asked was a necklace from my grandmother. It was a locket with a...I think my grandmother called it a cameo." He looked to Lenore, hoping a woman could confirm that he had used the right term. She nodded her validation.

He smiled slightly as he thought of his grandmother. "Bams was so...good to me. She spoiled me." A few more moments of thought elapsed before Jackson continued. "Anyway, she told me that the picture on that carved piece of shell was actually one of my grandmothers from the Isles. She had a big, long story about her grandmother falling in love with some Italian sailor who had decided he'd had enough of the sea. The sailor carved the cameo and gave it to her. But, her father, I guess it would've been one of my grandfathers, decided to find a new life here in America, and he took his family with him. That locket traveled across the ocean and stayed with her, even when she found someone new. Come down through our family. My mother told me she didn't think the whole story was true, but even though Bams was an older lady, I tell you what, you could see the resemblance between her and the woman in the locket." Jackson's attention had wandered. He began to think about Bams, his grandmother.

This led him to memories of his grandfather, Daniel Lee, who had died when he was just eleven years old. Jackson could see himself, around the age of eight or nine, walking through the woods on the top of a high ridgeline in the darkness of the early hours. His grandfather was walking with him. Down through a hollow they went until the land leveled off. They sat on the downhill side of a large oak at the edge of the bench that gave a view of the lower part of the ridge. The watch overlooked a path that his grandfather told him deer had been running since long before he, himself, was a boy. The path led up to a stretch of thick evergreens where the deer liked to bed down during the day. The head of the trail started at the perimeter of an abandoned farm, one that he told Jackson had been deserted so long ago that the locals believed the family had been killed by Indians. No one really knew for sure.

They waited there for a few hours. The sun had risen, and the forest was quiet, save for an occasional bird calling out, or a gray squirrel running through the leaves on the ground. Jackson's grandfather had whispered in the boy's ear that they would walk up through the pines and try to kick something out on their way over the ridge top and back to their own farm. They stood up and instantly froze. Fifty yards down the path, a large forked-horn had raised his head up. They stared at each other for a quarter of a minute. The deer began to slowly slink up the path, unsure of what he had seen or heard. Jackson's grandfather slowly handed his old muzzleloader to the boy, who looked at his grandfather with a little bit of confusion. Tall for his age and preternaturally strong, he held the gun steadily, but still wondered why his grandfather had given it to him. His family depended on wild meat to survive, and his grandfather was the best shot for miles around. The old man just nodded and stared back at him in a manner that told the boy it was his shot to take. With that, Jackson hesitated no more. He took it. As the smoke from the powder cleared, the boy did not look to the deer, to see if he had hit the buck. He looked to his grandfather. No words were spoken, but pride shone on the old man's face. Jackson instantly knew that he had made the shot. His grandfather turned away to look at the deer. "God provides our talents, but then we must make our way." He turned back to Jackson. "You have a fine eye, Jackson." The boy was never sure what his grandfather was talking about, but he knew from the tone of his voice that there was pride. And Jackson was proud of himself. After that day, he became a hunter. He always made the shot it seemed, but he made it his mission to learn the art of hunting the game. It was the one thing he could beat his brothers at. Before he stopped his schooling, it was something everyone knew about him. He did not know much about reading and writing, but he knew all he needed when it came to providing for...

It's all right, Jackson. Take your time." She patted his thigh.

"Mmm. Oh. Umm." Jackson shook his head as if a shiver had run up his spine. "The cameo. Bams gave it to me...gave me the cameo...to give to Annabel. And you should have seen..." Jackson quickly thought that he probably should not say how beautiful she looked to Lenore a second time. "Well, I loved her reaction. Tears welled up in her eyes. She couldn't stop smiling. She was just...mmm. When she said she loved me, it was the happiest I'd ever been.

"We got married in the fall of '60. Bams died not too long after that. Pretty selfish to think, but it seemed like she had felt she was done on this Earth. All her grandkids were grown. Me marrying Annabel was the last one to go." Jackson absentmindedly pictured his grandmother one last time. He had always been jealous of his brother, Galen, who could tell such great stories. Jackson always seemed to lose focus, daydream, or go off on tangents. With a shake of his head, he said, "Tried having kids." Jackson laughed. "Tried a lot." Again, he wondered how honest he should be. Why had he not waited till morning to propose? Yet, something had a hold on him now. Years had passed since he had last thought of these things. They did not seem so dark anymore. These memories actually brightened his spirit. "You know, the best way to describe it was touch." Lenore looked at him oddly. "I could tell you how beautiful I thought she was, but that wasn't it." He thought of something he had discovered about his wife in the first year they were married. "Sometimes, when I looked in her eyes, the rest of the world just disappeared. I mean it was like a spell had been cast on me. Every time I heard her voice it felt like someone was calling me home. But, the best thing was her touch. Holding her hand. Her kiss. Just putting my hand on her shoulder or the back of my hand across her cheek. In our small cabin, I might accidentally bump into her…and it felt so right. And when she would touch me, it was…it was like a warmth spread through me. It wasn't as though her touch was hot or anything. I just mean there was…I don't know…I could feel her love for me." Jackson's mind had become so focused that for a moment he had forgotten Lenore was there. As he paused to try to sort through what he had said, her presence came back to him. He looked at her and said, "Does that make any sense?"

"Yes," was all she replied. There was only silence for a long time. Jackson slowly grew agitated. Although he was glad to actually think about Annabel again, he knew that the story was about to grow dark and cold. With a deep sigh, he stepped into the storm.

"Well, I've told you about signing up. No need to repeat all that. My brothers joined first. If I was going to go, I wanted to go with them. Besides, neither one of them could shoot straight. Annabel stayed behind on our small piece of land. She tried to keep our place going, but come winter, she moved in with my folks.

"You know we all thought the war would be over in that first year. Then another year goes by. Next summer, after that, there's the fight here. Both Galen and Byron got killed. Thought that was about as low as

I could go. But, naw, I didn't know anything yet. My mom passed on. I really think...I mean, I know her heart was broken. It just gave out. That winter my father went out hunting one day. Got lost in a storm. Froze to death. Thing is, that man could find his way home with a blindfold on. Can't say for sure, but I reckon he'd had enough of this old world. Just decided to sit down and let the cold and the good Lord take him. Both times I got them letters from home it was a shock. But, I still had Annabel. I just wanted to get back to her. Didn't matter if I had to kill every bluecoat Billy Yank in Lincoln's army, I was going to end that war and get home to my wife." He stopped, swallowed hard, and then said, "And then she was gone too.

"See, come the end of winter that year Annabel had decided to leave my folks place. Just couldn't keep it going. Gettin' low on food, provisions, and such. Didn't have no help to plant that spring. Don't think there were any slaves in the county I was born in let alone up the hollow where our home was. So, her letter told me she had parceled out the few livestock we had, and then she left Virginia. Annabel had some kin down near Charleston, down in the Carolinas. Went to see them. While she was there she went to work with this doctor, treating all the boys that had been wounded. She didn't have no training like your Mahlon, but she was good at it. You could tell in her letters that she was proud of the work she was doing. Said she finally felt like she was helping in some small way. Maybe not directly, but she felt like she was helping me. Imagine that."

Both Lenore and Jackson did. Again, a tenuous silence came over the room. Images of terrified and maimed soldiers, struggling to come to grips with their wounds filled Lenore's mind. Jackson's thoughts were only of his wife. When he could no longer stop himself from thinking about her, he always saw one vision. It was of her in a hospital. He could only ever see over her shoulder as she comforted a young soldier, too young to have been in a battle, but horribly wounded all the same. The soldier was clear to him. The blood soaking through bandages on his upper chest and his left hip always drew Jackson's attention. Finally, he would reach out for his wife, yet that ethereal form was eternally beyond his reach. His mind would go no further. Her face, her beautiful, angelic face was lost to him forever.

"You said Mahlon's death extinguished the light inside you." Lenore nodded. "For me it wasn't light." He struggled to find a way to explain it. "It was time. And I didn't lose it." Jackson shook his head slightly from side to side as if trying to refuse it all over again. "I had too much of it. You know how when you were a kid on a sunny, summer day. That day just seemed to last forever; running and playing, swimming and laughing? It seems like the day's never going to end. When it does, you're so exhausted you just fall right to sleep. Wake up and it's another long, sunny day ahead of you. Now imagine that day with no sun, no laughing, nothing. And it just won't end. You're exhausted right from sun up. And when the night comes you can't sleep, because when you sleep...Well, you just can't sleep." He closed his eyes. Guilt washed over him. Jackson wanted to feel that emptiness again, if only to punish himself for daring to speak her name.

For the first time, Lenore wondered if she had gone too far in asking Jackson to reconnect to his wife and face up to her death. It had been done out of her love for him, but now she understood that just because facing up to her husband's death helped her heal and move forward, did not mean that it would work for Jackson. She told herself that she should stop this. They could still get an hour or so of sleep. Yet, something restrained her from letting Jackson stop. She had to know the end of the story. Jackson had never explained any of it, and the void of information felt like a sharp stick poking Lenore in the ribcage. Her mind told her that it was wrong to ask, yet she did. It almost seemed like someone else was asking. "What happened to her, Jacks? What happened to Annabel?" Lenore did not realize it, but by simply asking a question she had pulled Jackson back from a dark abyss.

He answered her with a deep sigh and then matter-of-factly said, "A fever took her." Jackson quickly decided that he did not want to think about her anymore. "You might believe that being a soldier I would not have had time to think about her. But, we were encamped, still trying to recover from our losses here." Jackson said "here," but he pointed toward the northeast part of Lenore's bedroom. "Getting ready for a spring campaign. We knew the Yanks had a new commander. Damned if he ain't our new president." Jackson shook his head at the thought of that. "There hadn't been much fighting for us after the battle here.

Got the news about Annabel in camp. Got it in a telegram. Didn't even know she was sick. That's how fast it took her. Later on, her aunt sent me a letter trying to explain. Said they had given her a beautiful funeral with an expensive casket and tombstone. Mmm. I remember she actually wrote, "a beautiful funeral," like there is any such thing. A friend of mine, I told you about him, Sergeant McClintock, read it to me. Can't read too well anyhow, but even still, I couldn't bring myself to...to even look at it." Jackson stopped for a good ten seconds. "I'm sorry, Lenore. I really don't recall much from those days. It wasn't long after that we fought near Fredericksburg again, then Cold Harbor. All I remember is that it seemed like the days would never end. The minutes just seemed like hours. I swear each day felt like a decade. There are still days when I feel like I've lived about nine lives...like a cat I guess."

She placed a hand on his leg just to have a connection with him. "I know, Jacks. It's all right. You can..."

"No. No, you were right. Let me finish." He looked right at her with blazing eyes of determination. It was too intense and Lenore moved her eyes slightly, looking at his chest. "Like I said...time seemed to stretch out forever. All I wanted was to sleep, but even if Robert E. Lee himself had said, 'Private, we are assigning you to full-time sleep duty,' I would have been derelict. I wanted to sleep, but it wasn't cause I was tired. I just wanted the damn day to end. I kept telling myself, 'Maybe tomorrow will be better,' but it never was. I'd lie awake. Get up and walk around. Take on extra guard duty. Usually a hour or two before sunrise my body would give in. It seemed like only a few minutes had gone by and that damn bugle would sound. Most people would've been angry. I couldn't even feel that. Couldn't feel nothin'. Nothing, that's all I had. Didn't give a damn about the war. My friends couldn't do anything for me. Archie tried to help me. So, did Robert. I wouldn't listen to them. Couldn't hear 'em. God was nowhere to be found. Funny, I was raised a Baptist, but for some reason I didn't even call on God, never prayed once. I just couldn't feel anything. Even after the war, I got into some scrapes, but I felt no fear...or excitement. Had some crazy times with McClintock. Still felt empty. Once the sergeant decided to settle down, I came back here to revisit where my brothers died. Obviously, I didn't have a chance to do it when I was here the first time. Saw the old Hess farm, and I immediately thought it was the right thing for me. This was where I was meant to be. It was...what's the word...irony."

"Ironic."

Jackson looked at her with a curious expression. "Isn't that what I said?" was what he wanted to ask her, but instead he knew he should just continue. "And then I met you and Ellie. You were such a ray of light. For almost five years I hadn't seen the sun. You smiled at me as you passed by. You remember? I was fixing the fence."

"I do."

"Something just told me that I had to call on you. It was likely you were married, but even if there was no chance of courting, I had to see you again. And when I did I met Ellie. Her smile, it…How do I explain it? It took a little bit of the pain away, filled a little bit of the emptiness. Little by little, I didn't want the day to be done. I wanted more. I wanted the daylight to go on. Being with you…it brought me…peace. I'm over that war, even though it'll always be a part of me. And I haven't forgotten Annabel. I never will. But, I can move on. That's what you wanted to know, right? I can move on."

"Ask me again, Jacks."

"What?"

Lenore swung her legs up under her body and faced Jackson on the bed. "Ask me." He knew what she meant this time. Jackson got up from the bed and knelt in front of her.

"Lenore, I love you. I want to make a life with you. And I think Ellie needs some brothers and sisters. I love you. Will you marry me?"

The answer was "Private Jackson Lee of Virginia!" It made both Lenore and Jackson jump, for it was a booming, yet tortured voice. It was loud enough to wake the dead, yet so strained they would turn over in their graves and cover their ears.

"Jacks?" The glow was gone. A look of anxiety replaced it. Fear filled her eyes. "What was that?"

"Jackson Lee! We know you are in there! We've come for you, Lee!"

"Dred."

"What? Talk to me, Jacks. What's going on?"

"The war's finally caught up with me, darlin'." He looked toward the front of the house, where the sound had come from, and thought about running. Then Lenore reached out and took hold of his arm just above the wrist, and Jackson quickly dismissed the thought. He knew he could not leave Lenore and Ellie here alone. Nor could he run with them. They would never get away. In an instant, he made a hard decision. Yet, the choice did not really require much thought. The only thing he could do was face his pursuers, giving his new-found family the chance to escape into town. Perhaps, he thought, they might save him in return. Although Jackson had never met the man, he was sure Adams County had a sheriff. "Lenore," Jackson looked straight into her eyes and even in the dimness of the candlelight she could see the seriousness. "I need you to stay calm."

"Jacks, if there's one thing I learned helping them slaves on their way up North, it's that when a person says what you just did, there's no reason to be calm."

"You might be right, but for Ellie's sake, I need you to keep your head."

Lenore sat up straight and said, "Okay. What's going on?"

"Someone from my past is here." Jackson realized that was obvious after he said it.

"Secesh?"

Jackson shook his head. He did not like the term, but did not have time to remind Lenore why. "They're from the South. Yes."

"And what do they want?"

"Jackson Lee!" Even though it was the second time Lenore had heard the voice, it made her jump again. "The time has come!"

"Me. It appears."

"Why?" she asked with panic in her voice, calmness be damned.

"No time for that. I'll tell you later."

"But..." There was so many questions swirling around in Lenore's mind.

Jackson was not going to answer them. "Get Ellie up. When I go out..."

"Why would you go out?" begged Lenore with even more exasperation.

"Because he's right. It is time."

"Who's right? Time for what? Talk to me!" Tears had come back to her eyes.

"Look I don't know how dangerous this could be, but I want you to take Ellie out the back. If you think you can make it, head to the Weikert place. If there's too many out there, try to get to the root cellar without being seen."

"The root cellar? Why not the barn?"

The voice erupted again. "I grow weary of waiting, Lee! My timepiece says it is six minutes till

149

five. At five we burn the house if you are not standing in front of me!"

"They'll have someone watching the barn."

"But I..."

"Listen carefully," commanded Jackson. "In the root cellar, behind the canned peaches are three mason jars. They're clear."

With wide eyes she asked, "What's in them?"

"Lenore, I love you." He grabbed her shoulders. "Now stop asking questions!" She did not like his tone, but knew the situation demanded it.

"Okay," she said with a mixture of trepidation for what was coming and anger for how he had spoken to her.

"Hide in the cellar. Get those mason jars. Crouch down near the cubby hole to the right of the door. If everything's good, no one will search for you. Even so, light your lantern once you're in the cellar. Keep it in the hole where we keep the potatoes so they don't see the light. If someone comes in the cellar, let them go past you. Then you and Ellie throw those mason jars at the stone walls near them."

"Why?" She could not help herself.

"Cause there's good old mountain dew in them jars, darlin', all right? Pure shine."

"Jacks!"

"It was a great place to store...Looke we ain't got..."

"Time is almost up, Lee!" The walls of the house seem to vibrate with the demand.

"First the mason jars, then throw the lantern hard enough to smash it. Then run as fast as you can for the fields. There's still a lot of corn stalks to hide in." Jackson pulled on his pants.

Lenore's faith and years of training came out. "I can't do that."

"Look, Lenore, I love that you're a member of the Friends and all, but this ain't about you fightin' for yourself or your country. It's about Ellie." His left boot went on.

Right on cue, the little girl cried out. "Momma! Mr. Jacks!" She caught her breath and yelled "Momma!" once more, in a way that breaks your heart and makes you ready to fight at the same time.

"Time's a wasting, Lee!"

"I hear you, Dred! I'm coming out you son of a whore!" he hollered, but he did not look very intimidating hopping on one boot while putting on the other. Still, Lenore was shocked and even more frightened by Jackson's outburst than she was of the man outside. It was a side of him she had never seen before this night. Jackson held her by the shoulders and said, "I'm not asking you to fight, or fire a gun. I'm taking your guns. Just protect Ellie."

"Okay. You know I will." He shook his head in acknowledgement. And then threw on his coat. "But, what about Sheriff Streeter?"

"Who?" asked Jackson, squinting his eyes.

"Sheriff Streeter. You met him before."

"Right. Right. Right." Jackson pointed to the south and said, "Lives in Fairfield. Are you sure I've met him?

"Yes! He just lives down the road a piece. He comes by here every morning around five-thirty, six o'clock."

"Okay. I still have to go out there. If you think you can find the sheriff, fine, but you get Ellie to safety. That's the important thing."

"I won't let you down."

Jackson put his right hand on the back of her head and kissed her forehead. "Now go." She immediately stepped toward the door, but the fog of battle was already descending. "Wait!" She stopped, but he was following behind her and gave her body a little push. They both kept walking toward Ellie's room. The little girl cried out again, Momma!" "I'm coming, Ellie!" cried Lenore.

"Where are the guns you told me came home with Mahlon?" demanded Jackson.

"Downstairs, under the virginals," answered Lenore without thinking about the ramifications.

"The what?"

"The harpsichord!" she yelled, not sure if Jackson knew what that meant either.

"Right. Okay." He wanted to ask for more, but they had reached Ellie's room.

"They're on the floor, back behind it, underneath a tanned deer hide. I didn't think anyone would ever look there for them. I just couldn't get rid of them, being Mahlon's and..."

Jackson interrupted her. "Good. Okay. Good. After I go out front, wait a little bit for anyone they had at the back to come around to my side. Then you go." He went to kiss her face, but they both were moving and he only brushed her hair with his lips. Then she was gone, disappearing into Ellie's bedroom.

Jackson began descending the stairs when he heard, "Time's up, Lee! Looks like you're still a coward!"

"I was getting dressed, you low-lying, filthy dog!" answered Jackson as he reached the bottom of the steps. "It's not yet morning by my reckoning!" It was becoming clear to Jackson that he too had been waiting for this day. It was not something he had pursued, but the anger and resentment that he had kept buried in the dark places of his mind had always wanted this to happen. "Now I'm coming for you! How you like that, Dred?" Unlike the bedrooms, the bottom floor of Lenore's home had lots of windows. There was plenty of light coming from the torches men were holding in front of the farmhouse. Jackson quickly moved across the parlor, close to the wall, trying to not provide any kind of silhouette for the men outside. He recovered a Henry repeater and a Colt single shot from exactly where Lenore had said they would be. Fortunately, the ammunition was there as well. Jackson had not even thought to ask her about it. When he looked up from securing the weapons he was met with an image he had never taken notice of before. There on the virginal was an ambrotype of Mahlon, Lenore, and a small toddler, who was obviously Ellie.

Quietly, he said to the picture, "I'm sorry I brought this on your family, Mahlon. I promise I won't let anything happen to them. Ellie won't end up in that horrible orphanage over in Gettysburg."

As he turned to look out one of the windows, Jackson thought about what he had just said. It perplexed him. He could not recall ever seeing an orphanage when he was in town, let alone knowing if it was good or bad. He shrugged it off, believing that Lenore must have told him about it. There were more important things to focus on. From what passed as a parlor, he could see about eight men standing or sitting on horses. Jackson thought he saw movement in the shadows on the right. Perhaps there were nine. Many wore what appeared to be flour sacks on their heads with eyes cut out, or bandannas around their faces. From the house he recognized no one but the colonel, the one he called "Dred." He could not clearly see the other figure sitting on a horse, but he still knew with certainty who would be seated at the right hand of his commander.

There was no time for planning anything elaborate. The basic plan in his mind was simply to stall, hoping Lenore and Ellie could get away. Jackson knew he was outmatched when it came to wits, and apparently outgunned as well. His former comrades, now enemies, held almost all the advantages. Yet, Jackson realized it was time to face them. He simply tucked the pistol into his belt after checking the loads.

The barrel pointed toward his right leg. He held the rifle with his right hand. A deep breath escaped from his lungs as he opened the door and stepped into the darkness of the early autumnal morning.

Chapter 5

...because words can inspire and wound, but numbers, after all, rule the universe

As Jackson began walking towards them, he assessed the odds. There were the two men directly in front of him on horseback. He was familiar with their fighting abilities. They wore Confederate army jackets and hats. The leader, whose black horse was slightly in the foreground, wore butternut. It looked like that color came more from the age of the fabric than the intention of a dye. There was faded blue facing with gold trim on the sleeves and at the neck. Three stars adorned the collar. The other officer, with a slouch hat pulled low, kept his horse a step back and to the right. His uniform was cadet gray. Three gold bars on his collar told the story of why he stayed behind. A whale oil lantern held in the junior officer's left hand gave off an eerie glow, illuminating one side of each officer in a haunting, soft light. Knee high boots that looked more at home on cavalry officers were pushing on all four stirrups. Their weapons were apparently holstered, for Jackson could not see any guns in their hands, which were covered with embroidered gauntlets. Like their boots, the gloves seemed more akin to the cavalry. It all made Jackson wonder what his former comrades had been up to in the four and a half years since the war ended. Upon drawing within ten yards of them, Jackson confirmed the identity of both, but he chose to only address the leader. "Colonel Hildred Moray, been a long time."

With a subtle movement of his eyes, Jackson began to evaluate Colonel Moray's small band. To Jackson's left was a wagon hitched to one horse. A man with a hood over his head held the reins. Two smaller men, maybe boys, stood farther away on the other side of the wagon, hoods loosely fitting over their faces as well. Jackson could not see what was in the wagon, and that made him nervous. The man at the reins only held the horse. Again, there was no gun visible in his hands, but one of the smaller ones held a shotgun. The other young one did not appear to be armed. He only held a torch. Two men, with bandannas over their faces, stood on the other side of the mounted horses, to Jackson's right. They both held torches and guns. However, Jackson was not afraid of them either. It was rifles they held, and muzzleloaders at that. They would most likely have to lose the torches before they could fire on him, and it would only be one shot. Their sight would be poor after they ditched their torch. Jackson's eyes moved on and then immediately shifted back.

If not for a sudden flash of movement, Jackson would have missed one member of the small mob. There was somebody standing about thirty feet behind the group beside an old, barren apple tree, holding the reins of several horses. One of the mounts moved his head up and down a few times or Jackson would have never seen them standing there in the shadows. The light from all of the torches was not overwhelming, but it hid what lay beyond. There was no way to tell what sort of weapon the man in the shadows had. Finally, at the end of Moray's left flank, was another enemy short in stature. However, he only had a bandanna to hide his identity, and his eyes looked very young. Even in the low light of the individual flames, Jackson could see that the boy's eyes showed no experience in this sort of thing, but they did show eagerness and excitement. That worried Jackson a little because he too held a shotgun. Then Jackson saw an opponent that was even shorter. A mixture of white, gray, and brown fur, an old German bird dog, stood at the teenager's side, staring intently at Jackson and pointing as if he had found their prey all by himself.

"Never going to be enough time, Lee," responded Moray.

"Never enough for what?" asked Jackson with an edge of disgust.

"For me to forgive and forget the likes of you," spat the officer.

The colonel's voice was dripping with enmity. A reunion of old comrades was obviously not their reason for calling on Jackson, but he knew that already and continued to calculate the odds. The Confederates had, no doubt, pistols that were holstered. There could also be rifles in scabbards behind their saddles. Jackson could not see any sabers. They were still infantrymen despite their horses and mixed accoutrements. Two other adults had old rifles. Two boys had shotguns. And there was the mystery man in the shadows who had his hands full with horses. Perhaps, they did not have as many advantages as Jackson first thought. "What do you want with me? The war's long over."

"Look yonder and see." The colonel's arm stretched out, pointing far behind the farmhouse. Jackson followed the direction of the gesture and found himself staring at his own home upon the rise. There in front of his house stood a fiery cross.

He slowly turned back to the colonel. Jackson's calmness surprised everyone, including himself. "I'd heard some things 'bout General Forrest still raisin' Cain."

"You misinterpret the symbol, Lee. Of course, you never were too bright." Moray looked at the men around him, as though making sure they were paying attention. He was about to show his vast knowledge. "You see that is not a Latin cross. No sir. That is the cross of Saint Andrew. It is a call to war."

"There is no war, Dred. We lost. You lost." Jackson was not sure if his next sentence came from a tactical thought or simply malice. "And so did that snake son of a bitch beside you." Jackson slightly dipped the barrel of his rifle in the direction of the small man on a white horse. He still wore the uniform of rebellion. Unlike Moray's, it looked freshly laundered and pressed. His entire manner looked sharp. From the crispness of his hat's brim to the fine lines of his dark goatee and mustache to the polish of his boots, the officer exuded military bearing. And that is exactly how Jackson remembered him. Every time he saw Moray's chief of staff, there was a cold steel about him. His demeanor was only ever broken by a slight smile as he inspected the troops after a battle. It had always disturbed Jackson. Most officers showed some range of emotions, from true sorrow at the deaths of men in the prime of their life to a bursting pride in the swell of victory. This one only allowed a thin smile to show, no matter the outcome. The men in Jackson's squad began to call him "Old Scratch." They were not physically afraid of him, but he spooked them all the same.

"Why must you insult Captain Apallion?" pleaded Moray with mock indignity.

Jackson responded with a rude bluntness. "Because I don't trust that oily, Greek bastard." He stared down Apallion to make his point. The captain never blinked.

"You should have more respect, Private. He always worked tirelessly for you boys." The colonel paused for the briefest moment, but thought better of allowing a response. He continued, "Well now, Marse Robert may have surrendered, but I never did. The war will go on. And you, coward Lee, you will be coming back with me."

It was so audacious, so unexpected, that Jackson could do nothing but laugh. Then he realized that Colonel Moray was not trying to be funny. There was true rancor in the words. Jackson saw the demonic glare in his eyes, and in the briefest of moments remembered every battle Moray had led him into. Anxiety was what Jackson felt when he had stepped from Lenore's house. Now the anxiety was giving way to anger. "I gave all I could to the struggle. I won't give no more."

"You signed on to fight for Virginia and damn it, that's what you shall do!" insisted Moray, practically spitting venom.

"I fought cause my brothers joined up. Both of 'em died just a few miles from here. Byron bled out underneath a peach tree. Galen was shot in the head. They found him lying dead in some farmer's field of summer wheat. As for me, I was wounded two times. Course you wouldn't remember that. Now I can't walk straight cause of my hip. Can't hardly toss a fork a hay cause my shoulder. Now you're telling me I didn't bleed enough for the Old Dominion. Ain't that somethin'. I believe you best face your demons on your own. I've learned to live with mine."

"We all lost something in that war, but most of us didn't turn yellow like you." Moray's chin was suddenly raised and a look of revelation came over his face. "That reminds me; you were no good after your wife died. Captain Apallion, what did dear Annabel die from?"

Before the captain could answer, Jackson said, "I'm warning you, don't."

"I do believe, Colonel Moray, it was the Yellow Jacks that took her." The captain tilted his hat up just enough for Jackson to see his eyes in the eerie glow of the lantern. They were almost gleeful. "A most interesting coincidence," he said in a low, smooth voice. A sly, sinister smile came over the junior officer's face.

"That's right, the fever took dear Annabel," confirmed Moray. "The Yellow Jacks, how appropriate that is in retrospect," he said in a haughty manner. In a flash, Jackson had the rifle up and pointed in the direction of the Confederate officers.

"Speak my wife's name again and I shoot you first."

"Calm down, Private Lee!" ordered Moray. "There may be a little blood tonight, but no one needs to die."

"No one ever needs to die. They just seem to do it a lot around you."

"I must say, Private Lee. I don't remember you being so quick witted. Sergeant McClintock must have taught you a few things. Where is the good sergeant by the way?"

"Haven't seen him in years," answered Jackson honestly. "And if you're here for the rumors of the gold his brother stole, I've got news for you. That was just a legend. We looked for it. There weren't none. But the sergeant did teach me a few things about you while we were traveling around. He set me right, that's for sure."

"Ain't that something?" asked the colonel in a faux hillbilly accent, for he was as highbrow as they came. "Maybe someday you and the good sergeant will enlighten us with tales of your adventures." Moray paused and just stared at his former enlisted man, hoping he would take the cue and tell more about what he had done after deserting. Jackson would not comply. "Well, as I was saying, General Forrest and his invisible empire are trying to restore the rightful order of things, but I am on a more personal mission. I am here for you. Next, will be McClintock. We will gather everyone who abandoned our cause, and then we will strike at the heart of our enemies. We will cut off the head of the snake, and this time we will complete the mission, unlike those fools did with Lincoln. To quote the devil, 'My great concern is not whether you have failed, Private Lee, but whether you are content with your failure.' You see, I am not content with our failure. And I am certainly not content with yours."

"Sorry, Dred. You'd have to kill me before I'm a part of any of that." The rifle had slowly gone down, but now Jackson began to raise it up again.

Colonel Moray looked to his chief of staff and sighed. They nodded to each other as if there was some telepathic connection, and they had just agreed on a new direction. "If that is the way it must be, Private Lee." The colonel maneuvered his horse over to the side of the wagon. "Either way," he said. Then he pulled a burlap covering off the cargo in the wagon. "You're coming with me." Suddenly, Jackson realized that despite Colonel Moray's previous proclamations, this had been the plan all along. He was here for revenge, not some crazy idea of southern honor, fighting to the last man, and killing some snake, whatever that meant. In the wagon, just visible above the sideboards, was a coffin, or more accurately, a casket. Strangely, it was not a plain pine-box. It was rectangular in shape and looked to be made of hardwood with ornate handles.

The sight of it unnerved Jackson, but he could not explain why. He had seen more than his share of death. A coffin should have the same impact as seeing a bat flying in the twilight, spooky to some, nothing to him. Yet, his eyes were frozen, drawn to the smooth lid. It was so out of the ordinary that Jackson wanted to stop the demented give and take with Moray, simply to go look at the coffin more closely. Only a few seconds passed before he realized that was not possible. The spell was broken by nothing more than the nurturing feeling he felt for Lenore and Ellie. Jackson knew that the longer he talked the better chance they had to get away. He had to keep up the bluster. "Someone's going to die, but it ain't me."

"You are quite feisty tonight," said Moray with a devilish smile. "Yet, as slow as you once were, I'm sure you're a smart enough soldier to realize you're outmanned and outgunned."

"Well, that might depend on who these boys are." Jackson made a point of looking them over. "Let's see what they can do when the bullets start flying."

"You're right Private Lee. Let me introduce you, so you know just how alone you are. These gentlemen are your neighbors here in...Captain, what county is this?"

"Adams, sir," answered Apallion.

"Ahh, probably named for that abolitionist scum, John Adams. Mmm. Back to your neighbors. These men have simple interests. Cale here wanted that land you bought after the war. You swept in and bought it out from under him."

Cale Baumgartner, a farmer and apple grower, was stunned to hear him be singled out. Standing immediately to the colonel's left; he turned to Moray and through his bandanna said, "You said we weren't going to use names." He sounded completely exasperated.

"So I did Mr. Baumgartner," responded Moray, but he never gave it a second thought. "As I was saying, Lee; old man Hess was going to sell to him before you came and, by my understanding, made a ridiculously generous offer. Perhaps your legendary adventures with Sergeant McClintock had something to do with that. There may be more truth there than you let on."

"You lie." That was all Jackson could or wanted to say, but he said it with force. Every man there heard him clearly.

Ψ

In the back of the house, Ellie heard him as well. Lenore and Ellie now crouched down and pressed themselves against the rear wall of their home. Ellie was bundled into her winter coat. Lenore wore a light jacket she kept for autumn and spring weather. In Lenore's right hand was an unlit lantern. She had grabbed it as she exited out through the pantry, hoping she would not have to attempt what Jackson had directed her to do. She could barely remember what he had said. Even if she could, it sounded too complicated, too much for her to accomplish. Beyond that, they faced a more immediate dilemma. Jackson had proved prophetic. There was, what appeared to be, a young man standing in front of the barn. He stood sentry, holding what looked to be a shotgun across his chest.

Looking from the front of the house, the barn stood to the rear left. The family's outhouse had been dug farther beyond it. Directly behind the house, in the middle, was a corral. To the right and rear of the house was the root cellar. There were places to hide, but to get to them meant crossing open ground. There were no bushes or trees right behind Lenore's house. She crouched down, holding Ellie's hand, not sure of what she should do. There were the fields out beyond the corral and root cellar. Back behind the barn and outhouse was a small woods. The guard had been posted in front of the large doors of the second floor of the barn. The road that led to their home terminated on a short incline leading up to those doors. Inside was a considerable amount of hay and some straw, along with the family's wagon. The first floor, which was made of stone, contained the stables for their three horses and five dairy cows. Lenore could see that one of the horses had gotten out of their stable and had come out into the corral, which was connected to the lower doors in the middle of the barn's stone foundation. In the darkness she could not tell which horse it was. It seemed quiet, which probably meant it was the old roan they called Big Red. Even if they could get to the horse, Lenore knew that Red did not possess enough speed to outrun what were, apparently, Confederate soldiers on horseback. At least that was how it seemed as Lenore had quietly led Ellie out of their house. She clearly saw two men on horseback, dressed up like they thought it was 1863 all over again. Red would not be fast enough to outrun either of them.

She was sure of that. The two younger and faster horses were still in the barn, out of reach of Lenore and Ellie. Lenore was trying to simultaneously watch the sentry at the barn and listen to what was going on out front. Lenore could only make out a few words. Ellie heard everything, but could not understand what it all meant.

Ψ

"Walter and his boys here, and the young one out back, are interested in the gold you have," he whispered it like a secret, but it was pure sarcasm. "It appears their dry goods store is failing and their farm isn't producing." The colonel pointed to the three on his right with a torch, a shotgun, and the wagon's reins filling their hands. Walter was obviously the one holding the reins. "The Yankee gold you and your friend, McClintock, came into when you deserted after Cold Harbor would go a long ways toward helping them. It was from the North and to a northerner it shall return."

"All lies." Jackson said it forcefully in Walter's direction. He was busy shaking his head and adjusting his hood. Briefly he picked it up as if he just wanted to get a clean breath of air. Then it was replaced. That was enough. The colonel, Jackson realized, had not been lying about everything. It was indeed Walter Huber, who owned a store and farm to the north on the old Carlisle Road. It was truly disappointing because Lenore knew this family. Huber's wife had left the Quakers to marry him, but Lenore's mother, Maria, had continued to be friends with them. In fact, Lenore and her mother would take Ellie to visit them, especially after the mother went away to a hospital in Philadelphia. They had a fourth son, who was just slightly older than Ellie. He had been born with deformed legs. Little Ellie had befriended him. It seemed Moray had been right. Revealing to Jackson who he was facing made him realize that he had not become a member of the community in the time he had been in Adams County. There were no real friends to call upon. Jackson had not even bothered to join a church. This was Adams County, Pennsylvania. The county seat was Gettysburg. He was a former Confederate soldier. For all Jackson knew, he may have killed someone who had kin in this area. No one here was going to help him. He was alone. The knowledge of that was like a dam buster, and adrenaline began to flow out of his system. Jackson could feel the sharp edge of his senses growing duller

"Heinrich here, and his son, Manny, just don't like the fact that your whore is a nigger-loving jezebel who brought their black filth to Adams County." And just like that, the spell was broken.

"Damned lies." Moray had overplayed his hand. Insulting Lenore had quickly snapped Jackson out of his momentary disillusionment. He was not alone. Lenore and Miss Electa were everything to him now. That was why he would make his stand if needed. He had to give them the opportunity to escape. Jackson let go of the rifle with his left hand, then pulled the pistol from his waistband. "First you insult my wife. Now you insult Lenore. You ain't worthy enough to clean her outhouse, you wretched scoundrel."

"Damn it, Moray. You said we wouldn't use names," blustered the one called Heinrich as he pulled down his bandanna. His son followed suit. Jackson did not recognize him or his voice. That only mattered for another second.

"Might as well…might just take these damn hoods off. Can't see nothin'," stammered Huber. The two boys struggled to look tough, trying to pull off their hoods while trying to keep the torch from catching something on fire and the shotgun trained on Jackson. "Don't know why we wore 'em if you were just going to tell Lee our names anyway." With that, Baumgartner gave in and uncovered his face as well.

"It does not matter. For Private Lee is not going to remain here, nor return. There will be no witnesses to tell of the events of this night." The local hooligans and schemers did not catch the warning evinced by Moray's words. "The die has been cast by Private Lee. He has crossed the Rubicon and cannot go back." The references to Julius Caesar were completely lost on the locals and Jackson. Moray looked around, quickly realized his knowledge of classical Rome was wasted on them, and frowned in the direction of Captain Apallion. "Justice will be done. Land returned to the rightful owners. Yankee gold will be taken from the brigand who stole it. That is why you are here. I simply want Private Lee. His land and gold are yours. There is no going back. The common man shall rise again against the oppressors in Washington. And if blood must be spilt for the cause then let it flow freely."

Jackson had had enough. "But it's never your blood, and I mean to change that." His anger began to boil into a rage. He held his fire, but could not hold his tongue. "And don't you boys be calling Lenore a whore no more! She's a better person than all y'all in the eyes of God and man. All her family did was help some runaway slaves get through the county. And Dred, you're just angry cause she helped take away your negroes. People like you lost all your field hands, so you sent people like me out to fight for 'em. We were like sheep thrown to the wolves, but you didn't care! Common man?" Jackson tilted his head and repeated his question in disbelief. "Common man? What do you know of us? All you wanted was blood and ruin! You think I didn't ever see the look in your eyes before a battle? It was like a husband on his wedding night. The anticipation must have been almost too much for you to bear! And when it was all done and our boys were shot through, screaming to see their mama's face just one last time, you didn't shed a tear. You just smiled, same as 'Old Scratch' there beside you." Moray was smiling wickedly now. His blood was up just thinking about the images Private Lee had invoked. Jackson ignored him and his aide, choosing to stare down all the men on the ground.

"You boys best think 'bout that before this fight starts."

Jackson looked at each one of them individually, pausing every time to make sure they had eye contact. He asked, "Which one of you boys is going to go first? He'll be smiling when you do. Make no mistake; I won't die easy. How many of you have killed men?" Though friends with none, Jackson was sure he knew the answer. None of them had served in the war. He could tell just by the way they held themselves, the way they held their weapons. "I have, and I will again, to protect Lenore and her little girl, Ellie."

"He speaks the truth, boys. Private Lee is a born fighter. Well, that was till he went soft and became a regular, old Sunday soldier. Before that I was very proud to have him under my command."

"You didn't even know our names," shot back Jackson. "I might not be the smartest of men, but I know we were just pieces on a chessboard to someone like you."

"I am hurt," replied Moray with a flourish. An anguished look came over him. "I knew my men very well. Why, it was me that sent you a fine bottle of whiskey when your young wife died. You treat her name as if she'd been canonized, but what would she think of you now? Oh, the shame of it all. Her husband come to be a coward, shacking up with some heretic. Society of Friends? Seems to be more like a society of cowards. Those who would seek to abolish the world's rightful order. Annabel must..."

With a speed that astonished the local men and boys, Jackson raised the pistol, took aim, and fired before his opponents even had a chance to bring their arms to bear. Moray's hat flew off, freshly ventilated at the top. The horse that was hitched to the coffin-bearing wagon began to fight against the reins, snorting and straining to be free. Two of the locals, Walter and one of his sons, quickly forgot that a fight might be starting and worked to restrain and calm him, going as far as to turn their backs on Jackson. Moray simply smiled, but it seemed that he was laughing at his recruits' lack of competence. Apallion never moved. Neither seemed worried by the fact that the men they had at their disposal had gotten their weapons trained on Jackson at the same time he was lowering his own. In truth, only the one called Heinrich and his son had even raised their guns. Baumgartner seemed stunned and Huber's other boy, the one with the shotgun, had jumped back at the report of the Colt. He seemed confused, looking at Jackson, then his father and brother, and then Moray.

"Calm down, boys. Private Lee, if I recall, was a superb marksman. He was simply firing a shot across the bow. I have no doubt that if he had wanted to kill me, he would've done so." Jackson, ever so slightly, nodded twice as if to signal that the colonel was correct.

"I told you not to say my wife's name again." He did not explain that the real reason he fired the shot was simply to test the loads in the Colt and the resolve of the men, not to mention if the weapon was sighted in.. It made no sense to start a gunfight if your gun was not working. The ammunition passed the test. Moray's men did not. As for the rifle, the standardized rounds in the Henry repeater would have to be trusted.

Moray shifted in the saddle, turning his face to each of the men. "I won't mention your wife again, Private, but the time has come. Get in the front of the wagon, Lee. Or you will be put in the back."

Ψ

Lenore and Ellie had jumped when the shot was fired. The mother had let a small yelp form, but she caught it before it became a full scream. At the same time, she covered Ellie's mouth, which was unnecessary. The little girl had made no sound. The young sentry named Terence had not noticed them anyway. He had been looking down, kicking at the dirt, angry with his father that he had been placed on guard duty in front of the barn. The lack of action had driven him to distraction, and when the shot was fired, he was spooked and jumped. The shotgun in his hands was almost fired accidentally. After recovering his sense of awareness, he just stood there, not sure what to do. By the time Colonel Moray commanded Jackson to get into the wagon, Terence had decided that he would best serve his father's interests by circling around to the front. It was clear that no one was trying to escape by way of the barn.

Lenore could not hear all of Colonel Moray's demands, but Ellie, with a heightened sense of hearing, got every detail. The words and the voice and the loud gunshot scared her. In a whispered tone, Lenore asked her daughter what the man had said. Quietly, Ellie explained, "He wants Mr. Jacks to go with him. He wants him to get in the wagon. Momma I know…"

"It's okay, Ellie. Jacks knows what he's doing. He's not like us in that way. He knows how to fight." Lenore looked again to the man at the barn. He had not seen them, but she knew that she could not cross the open space to get to the stalls. She was also afraid to try to get to the root cellar. They were trapped, huddled at the foundation, cursing something Lenore had always loved, a full moon. Then her prayers seemed to be answered. The sentry began to walk forward, going around the far side of her home. Lenore and Ellie were free to move. They could get to the barn and the faster horses. If it was too dangerous to get the horses riled up and possibly draw attention to themselves, then they could head out through the fields on foot. The Fairfield Road was just over one hundred yards away. Yet, neither one moved in those directions. Lenore's fear for Ellie had been overwhelming, but now she could not walk away from Jackson.

From the way he reluctantly told her stories and some of the things he mumbled, and even cried out, in his sleep, she had begun to think her sweet, loving Jackson had once been involved in some terrible, terrible things. He was a hardened fighter. This she had come to know with certainty, but Lenore had heard a number of voices on the other side of her home. How many did he face? When she had left the house, she had hoped it was only three or four. Now, from the different voices, she knew there was likely twice that amount. She could not run away. Instead, she led Ellie toward the root cellar. They could duck down into the entranceway and be able to see part of what was happening out front. How they could help did not occur to Lenore. She just knew that she could not leave Jackson, not now.

Ψ

Enough time had passed that Jackson thought Lenore and Ellie would have made it through the fields and were now on their way up Fairfield Road. Still, he wanted to stall as long as he could. Unfortunately, he was running out of things to say. Jackson had been in plenty of fights, but there had never been any insults or taunting, only anticipation, anxiety, attack, and anger. When it was over and all the fear was alleviated, he would collapse into an amalgam of relief, sorrow, and guilt. Talking never played a role in any of his battles. Essentially out of things to say, Jackson tried to keep the dialogue going, but it was not to be. "I'm not going nowhere with..." Action was craved by others as well.

"Why we all talking?" a voice from Jackson's right asked loudly. "M'tired of listening to this blowhard!" There was violence in the question he heard, and so before Jackson had even begun to turn his head the barrel of Mahlon's pistol had begun to rise up, sweeping to the right. The heavy, Colt single-shot felt good in Jackson's hand despite him using it for the first time only a few minutes earlier. The weight and balance felt right. By the time he saw the boy pointing his shotgun at him, the decision had already been made. Any thought of holding back because it was a boy had no chance against the instinctual reaction of a former soldier. Still, the boy pulled his trigger first, but mortal mistakes can happen in many ways. This boy's blunder was his aiming for Jackson's head instead of the center of his body. The smaller target on top of

Jackson's neck was moving as he turned. It was not a terrible shot by the boy, but it was off enough that his enemy would not be felled by it. The boy, or his father, had made another mistake. His gun was loaded with bird instead of buckshot. A few pellets hit Jackson in the upper chest, one hit his neck, and another tore through his ear lobe. The man who had known so much violence unleashed more at the same moment the shot ripped into the cartilage of his ear. The pain of the impact from the pellets made him drop the Henry rifle, but the Colt roared to life again. Jackson had aimed dead center on the boy's upper body without even thinking. The bullet ripped into his chest just to the left of his heart. It shattered a rib bone and tore into his lung. It came to rest there without leaving the body. The impetus of the bullet blew the boy back toward his father. Jackson pulled the trigger again, but nothing happened. He squeezed it once more, but the next chamber was as dead as the previous one.

"Manny!" The cry of distress from the boy's father was heard above the echo of the two gunshots. Not much else was. Jackson's ears were ringing from the sound of his pistol. Searing pain from his chest and neck was also distracting him. For a moment, he fought to focus only on the boy, who was prostrate before him. The sight of the father falling down beside the boy broke the momentary spell that had taken hold of Jackson. He was disgusted by the fact that he had shot a boy, but his experience in combat had control of him. Quickly he knelt down and picked up the Henry repeater and dropped the Colt. The burning sensation from his wounds was not enough to keep him from using the rifle. Jackson swung it up and pointed it at each of the different men standing before him.

Once more, Moray and Apallion had not moved. Cale Baumgartner seemed in shock. He stood rigid with his mouth open, fixated on the wounded boy. Jackson swung back to his left. He saw the Huber father staring at him with a look of horror in his eyes, trying to somehow come to grips with the fact that Jackson had just shot someone right in front of him, someone who was the same age as his own children. His two boys, Randolph and Arnold, were cowering behind the wagon. The mystery man with the horses had faded into the darkness, but Jackson could hear the horses nickering and snorting and kicking at the ground. Though it sounded as if they were far off, Jackson could clearly tell they were agitated.

And so was Jackson. The ringing in his ears was not abating. Multiple horses making all sorts of noises compounded the problem. The dog that had been at the boy's side was now barking, adding to the discordance. The man Moray had called Heinrich was now kneeling over the body of his son and practically wailing. "Said no one was going to get hurt. We were just going to scare 'em off. You said no one would get hurt!" It was clearly directed at the former Confederate officers, but neither one responded. Heinrich looked back at them with both dismay and hatred, but was too distraught to do anything. The devastation of the moment took hold of him. He turned away to focus solely on his only son. The colonel and his subordinate continued to stare at their former infantryman. Jackson briefly looked at the boy and noticed the short, quick breaths of someone struggling to get air. "You keep breathing, boy. Come on, Manny. I'm going to get you out of here." He began to slide his hands under his son's body, but at the same time the boy began to convulse and cough up frothy, bubbling blood. In a shocked reaction to the bloody spasm, the father pulled his hands away. "Don't die on me, Manny. You're all I got," he whimpered in a voice so low it could only be heard by his son and the dog. Coming from such a hard and unloving man, it was a truly unnerving plea. It made the dog go from barking to crying as if baying at the moon that was just now dipping low, ready to hide behind the ridge.

Ψ

At the root cellar's entrance, Lenore was struggling with the indecision that most people face when they are torn between fight or flight. She had the added disadvantage of being taught her entire life that war was wrong. This, she thought, was clearly war, or at least the echo of one. The bastards that had taken her husband from her had now come again. Was it not bad enough that some six years ago they had wreaked havoc on this beautiful land of South Central Pennsylvania and its people? Now they had come back to take Jackson from her. She had struggled, in her small way, for abolition, supporting her husband in his efforts with the Underground Railroad. Now abolition was the law of the land. Would she forever have to go on paying for that triumph? It was that question that made something change in her mind. As if a switch had been thrown, all of the vacillations left her. If she must pay then she would no longer let the toll be taken so easily. She would engage. "Ellie, duck down here child." Ellie felt the pressure of her mother's hands on her shoulders. She knelt down and leaned against the stacked field stone that lined the entrance to the root cellar. "I'm just going into the root cellar. I'll be back before your knuckles crack." Ellie liked to rhyme phrases.

Lenore usually enjoyed playing along with her. Now, it just brought a nauseating feeling to Lenore's stomach. This was not a game she told herself. "Just stay down, Honey." She kissed her on the head, opened the door slowly, and ducked under the low frame of the root cellar's door. The musty smell welcomed her into the darkness that only exists underground. Lenore hated to do it, but she closed the door, making it impossible to see her little girl for a moment. Quickly she struck a Lucifer. It blazed to life and as quickly as she could, operating by touch alone, she lit the lantern. With the door closed, no one would see the light. With rapidity, she scanned the shelves of canned goods. Mason jars were filled with peaches and plums, tomatoes, and peppers. There on the second set of shelves, near the top, she saw what she was looking for. Now could she use it to help the man she had come to love?

In a confused state of remorse and adrenaline, Jackson did what many men and women would do. He lashed out. "I didn't want this, Moray! This is your doing, you son of a bitch. You brought this on these folks! You had no right to get them involved in this.

There's no more fight! How long you going to hunt for people like me or Archie or McClintock? How many more gonna die?"

"As many as it takes!" Hatred seethed from the colonel. The genteel veneer had begun to crack. Jackson stared at Moray with such focused loathing that he barely noticed when Captain Apallion leaned over and whispered something to his commander. In truth, he may have spoken loudly, for Jackson's hearing had not returned to normal after firing the shot. "They came of their own free will, Private Lee. And you can end this right now by exercising your free will. Get in the wagon!" ordered Colonel Moray. The southern gentleman's calm demeanor was no more.

"You burn in hell. I'll never fight for you again." It was not Moray who answered this time, but Jackson recognized the voice, despite having not heard it in years. It addressed him with a nickname their platoon sergeant had bestowed.

"You have to, General. We can't let this keep going." At first, the image emerging from the shadows was ghostly in appearance, and Jackson thought it was some phantasm for the briefest of moments. "It ain't right what they've done...what they keep doing." The initial confusion began to break as Jackson recognized the tattered uniform of his old unit in the Army of Northern Virginia. After that, he wished it was an apparition. "Bad enough that my wife and kids went back to her kin in Georgia. And the Federals, they took all my stock. Didn't even leave me a horse. Even took Shadow, my old mare. You remember me telling you stories 'bout Shadow." Jackson did, and now that name brought only sadness, for here was a ghost, but only in the figurative sense. The friend he had known was gone, but Jackson's past would not let go of him. It would always haunt his soul. "Still weren't enough. They burned my farm, Jacks. Burned it all."

It was odd, but Jackson still asked, "Archie?" even though he had already recognized his friend's visage and voice.

"Now they got the niggers in power. It ain't right, Jackson. You know I never owned none of 'em. Now they treat me like I'm the slave. Now they're running things just cause they got old Billy Yank's guns backing 'em up."

"Why, Archie? Why would you ride with Moray and Apallion? You know what they are! They're everything we thought they were!"

Archie ignored his pleas. "Made 'em assemblymen, even congressmen in Washington. They weren't no better than cows and horses a few years ago. Now they're running the show? Me... I got nothing. I ain't got a damn thing!" A wailing cry from Heinrich interrupted the old comrades' reunion. He was sobbing, muttering, sounding like he was speaking to God in some dialect of German.

"This ain't the way," said Jackson, pointing to the dying boy and his bereaved father.

"It is. We're gonna cut off the head of the snake. That butcher, Grant, will get what's coming to him. All the traitors, like Longstreet, will get what they deserve."

"I can't be a part of that, Archie." Jackson's former friend did not respond. Archie had seen the boy coming. Moray and Apallion probably did as well. The civilians were too distracted by the guttural screams of a tormented parent, otherwise the old man Huber would have most likely told his son to stop what he was doing. Archie did not. He recognized the malice in the boy's eyes, but with a steely nerve that rarely comes from anything but combat, he did not betray the boy's approach to Jackson.

"I'm sorry, Jackson." Archie shook his head with a sad resignation. "You don't have a choice."

Terence had spun the old shotgun around. He held it by the barrel as he stepped quietly toward Jackson. He did not need to be so stealthy. Jackson's ears were still not back to normal after the gunfire. Horses whinnied and snorted. The father cried out for a dying son. It was a chaotic cacophony. However, the biggest reason he never heard Terence was the fact that Jackson never expected someone to outflank him. There was no anticipation of an attack from the rear, even though he had warned Lenore about someone being at the barn. The teenager took another step forward, raising his weapon up like a base baller's bat. The flat side of the shotgun's stock crashed into the rear right of Jackson's skull. The impact rang out. Expecting a thud, the boy was surprised by the loud crack that sounded in his ears. It probably would have killed a less stout man. Instead, Jackson flew forward, stumbling in silent pain. His sight was already gone by the time his first step hit the ground. A high pitched ringing from inside his head now became a full roar as if a forest fire was raging right by each ear. Though he could not see him, Jackson's addled brain somehow understood that he had fallen forward and hit his old friend, Archie. For a moment, Jackson stayed on his feet. He reached out to grab hold of Archie, but his brain was shutting down and his hand simply slapped against the former soldier's uniform. "Archie? Help...help me." Archie was momentarily stunned into paralysis and did not let go of the reins he held. Then he was scared for his friend, whose eyes began to roll back into his skull. Jackson awkwardly reversed direction, staggering two steps. He straightened to his full height for an instant, faltered, and sprawled backward, landing at the feet of his attacker.

Archie finally let go of the leather straps in his hands, not caring if all of the horses ran away. He went forward with cat-like quickness just as Terence was raising the shotgun above his head like an ax, ready to fall on freshly cut timber. The boy had a murderous look to him. Archie was smart enough to know he could not trust Moray completely. Perhaps this was his end game after all, but Archie had come to recruit his old friend, not kill him. He took hold of the boy's right arm just below the wrist. In a powerful, sweeping move he grabbed the barrel of the gun and swept his left leg through the boy's boots. Terence's legs flew up into the air. At the point when his body became horizontal, he released the gun into Archie's hands. The boy dropped a couple of feet and hit the ground, knocking the breath from him slightly. He looked up to see Archie break the gun, remove the shells, and close it again. With a speed too fast for Terence to react, Archie threw the double barrel down at him. It hit the boy square in the chest, bounced up, and cracked him in the face. Immediately it cut his cheek and gave him a fat lip, which also bled. With that, all the starch left the boy's body and mind. He was out of the fight.

The soldier knelt down beside his old comrade and checked to see that he was still breathing. "He's alive, Colonel," said Archie without looking up at the officer. "He's not going to be in too good a shape though."

"Don't you worry, Private Galloway, Lee's going to have a nice, long rest," Colonel Moray assured Archie. "Now you get him in that box, so we can ship him back. By the time he's home, he'll be ready to take orders again." He looked to Captain Apallion next. The soldiers that had once fought under the colonel's command would rise up again. They would be the catalyst for a renewed revolution from the South, and perhaps even more states from the West. Like a plague of locusts, they would swarm over these northern lands. They would bring on a destruction of Biblical proportions once Grant, their new commander in chief, was gone. And if they could not defeat the enemy in battle, then they would torment them with as much hellfire as possible until they gave up. These ideas; assassinations, robberies, even bombings, had been brewing in Moray's mind for four years. If they could not defeat the North on the battlefield, then they would bring terror to its population. Private Jackson Lee would come around. He just needed to be broken, much as Galloway had been. "But first, we must help poor Heinrich here." With a smoothness that comes from good breeding and the money for the best equestrian training, not to mention the horseflesh itself, the colonel dismounted his steed. Captain Apallion seemed to understand without a word being said. As soon as his boots hit the ground he was following his commander, holding the lantern as if to say that the colonel deserved more expensive lighting than mere torches.

Ψ

Lenore also had a lantern. She left it just inside the door of the root cellar, not wanting to draw any attention to her and Ellie. By the door, on the outside, she set down the mason jars. Ellie did not know what her mother was doing, but she hoped it was something that could help. For the first time, the little girl was becoming scared. "Momma, something's wrong."

"Why's that, Ellie? Why, Hon?"

"I can't hear Mr. Jacks anymore, Momma!"

Trying to calm Ellie, who was becoming louder than Lenore thought prudent, she rubbed her back and stroked her hair. "What do you mean?" she asked in a hushed voice.

"All of them other men are talking, but Mr. Jacks, he's not saying anything anymore. They said something about putting him in a box. Momma, what's happening?"

"It's going to be all right, Baby," but Lenore did not believe that. Despite being so innocent, neither did

Ellie. Yet, both of them could not think of what to do. Lenore tried to remember what Jackson had told her to do with the alcohol in the mason jars. She was having trouble recalling it all. The same thought kept coming back to her; she was not meant for this. There had never been any reason for her to fight. Ellie did not fully grasp the abhorrence of violence by some and the need to inflict it by others. She had a disadvantage in her blindness, but her family, and her natural disposition, had allowed her to see the world as she wanted to, a loving place. That was all she could do. Now she saw what she heard and knew there was more to this world. There was a darkness that had nothing to do with her blindness. Yet, she calmly realized there might be something she could contribute.

"Listen, Momma, please," begged Ellie.

"What child?"

"I know who's out there," declared the little girl. "I know that horse."

"What horse, baby? There's a bunch of them." Lenore was confused by it all.

"The one closest to us."

Ψ

The horses were highly agitated. Oddly, Moray and Apallion's now riderless horses remained calm, hardly moving. The two men in gray had seemingly left them behind without a care. As the confederate officers came up beside the father and his dying son, Moray removed his gloves slowly and deliberately. He surveyed the situation carefully, looking at the boy, then Archie, and then at Huber and his sons. Heinrich was quieter now. Convulsions racked his body. All he could do was sob. His son stared up into the night sky. The light of the torches and lantern danced on his face, making the frozen shock in his eyes stand out even more against the twirling light on his skin. Manny broke the silence that had fallen over them. "It's getting dark. I can't see, Daddy. I can't see. I'm dying, Daddy." His dog now lay next to him whimpering. Every few seconds he would push his snout into Manny's ribs and whine.

Heinrich tried to summon some courage for his son, but it was just ramblings. It made little sense. "Hush now, boy. It's going to be all right. It's going to be over soon. You're going to be just fine." Heinrich loved his boy but had never been able to show that. Nor had he ever tried to understand why he could not show or say it. Even now, with all of the anguish he felt over his dying son, there was also wrath. His son could be so full of joy one minute and then make Heinrich so mad the next. Even with the end near, the father was still so incredibly angry with his son. And despite knowing it was wrong, he could not keep his mouth shut. "You started this fight here, Manny. You wanted to be a man...now you got to die with dignity, son."

It was all too much for Cale Baumgartner. He turned away and began to walk into the night. As he left, he said to no one in particular, "Damn fool, expects a boy to know how to die. Ain't no dignity in dying no matter what." Not bothering with the road, he walked toward the large pond to the southeast of the house, in the opposite direction of his home, talking to himself the whole time. "Every one of us dies scared. Everyone dies for themselves, alone. Damn fools, that's all we've been." With that, he walked into the shadows. Colonel Moray watched him go but did not try to force his charge to return. Baumgartner was dead weight and useless in a fight. Yet, Cale's words ripped away any resolve Heinrich had been able to muster. Once more he wept. "Oh, son why? Why were you always starting fights? With me. With our neighbors. At school. I don't know where that temper came from. Your momma didn't have it. Oh, God. What would your momma think of me now? Done got my son killed."

Manny cried out, "Is Momma waiting for me, Daddy?" Blood spilled from his lips along with a gurgling of fluids. Losing strength, he began to whisper, "Is Momma gonna be there? I don't want to die, Daddy. I don't want to..."

The father looked up from his son and said to Moray, "Isn't there anything you can do?" Captain Apallion stared at him with no change in expression. His eyes showed an emptiness that anyone could see. Nor did Colonel Moray's twisted visage express empathy.

Moray answered him with a perturbed look instead. He sighed heavily and turned to his chief of staff. "Ahhh, damn it. None of you boys was supposed to die here. Captain Apallion, what is your opinion?" The junior officer rigidly nodded his affirmation. "All right then, first things first. Mr. Huber!" Huber and his two older sons looked shocked to hear their names. "You and your sons..." Moray suddenly stopped his order. Even he was somewhat taken aback that Huber and his two sons had not yet lifted a finger to help the third son, Terence. He shook his head a little and continued the order. "You will place Private Lee in the box in the wagon. Make sure it is locked once he is in it. Understood?"

"No, sir. My boys and me don't want no more parts of this!" Mr. Huber was adamant.

Moray coldly stared into the man's eyes. He let the man's imagination grow. Finally, he said, "Walter, do you really want to become a deserter?"

"I'm...I'm not...not a soldier," Huber stammered.

"That is very clear, but you would be a deserter nonetheless. Can't you see what happens to deserters?" The hand holding his two gloves swept across to Jackson's body. He turned back to Huber, hoping the man was too scared to think about Baumgartner leaving moments earlier. "You have my orders, Mr. Huber." The man held onto his independence for a few more seconds.

"Let's go, boys." Moray's lip began to snarl but was quickly relieved. "Get him up in that wagon. C'mon!"

"Private Galloway!" shouted Moray.

The response was quick and obedient. "Yes, Colonel."

"Take charge of that detail."

"Does he actually need to be in the box?" Moray was growing livid, but still managed to regain some of his calm demeanor. He told himself he was a leader, and could not demonstrate any lack of control. Still, he would need to deal with this lack of military bearing.

"Yes, Private Galloway. He doesn't remember what it means to lose like you do. What this war did to us is not fresh enough in his mind." Moray was pleased with his off-thecuff answer, yet he could not help but be distracted by the Huber family's behavior. They walked over to Jackson's prone body, still ignoring the other member of their family, who remained on the ground. He was bleeding from two points of his face, and there appeared to be tears welling up in his eyes. For a short time, Moray studied the youngest Huber son, that he recalled being named Terence, while watching the men and boys in his peripheral vision picking up Jackson. "And, Private, once you are done with Jackson, recover all the horses. The Hubers will help you." It was clear from their submissive movements that his orders would be followed. Moray turned and walked over to the dying boy whose breaths were strangled and intermittent. He knelt down and said, "Mr. Rotz, Heinrich, I need you to stand. Let my friend, Captain Apallion, help your son."

"What are your orders, sir?"

"Captain Apallion, do you remember the lessons we learned from Mother Amie Arête Ankou, that Vodoun priestess down Louisiana way?"

"I do, Sir," affirmed the captain.

"Remind me, Captain Apallion. Who do I call on?"

"A Loa, Sir. Draw on the power of the Loa."

"The harvest prayer if I recall, dying in the fall, reborn in the spring, and all that."

"Yes, Colonel. Amie prayed to Aida-Wedo and the full spectrum of the world. Many others are drawn to the serpent, Danbhala-Wedo." The boy's father stared at both of them with an intensity born of fear. Wide eyes were filled with trepidation, but he needed their help. Desperation had overtaken him. Yet, he had no idea what they were talking about, and that scared him even more than he already was.

"A fine woman, Mother Amie. A fine woman she was, a credit to her race, or races if you please." Moray pulled the grieving father to his feet. The colonel's free hand was placed on his shoulders. Both Rotz and Moray stared directly at the junior officer.

"For life to be given, life must be taken," said Apallion.

"Yes. Yes. I would die for…"

The captain cut him off. "Noble, but not necessary. Face the moon and listen to the colonel. Do not turn back until your son speaks again." The colonel turned him around. Their eyes locked onto the pale, autumn moon.

"Now, Mr. Rotz, you listen to me, and the prayer I offer. The second time you will say it with me. Do you understand?"

"Yes. Yes. Anything. Please hurry."

Colonel Moray had seen many things in his life, and some of them he could not explain. Whether him raising his gloves toward the moon helped or was simply theater, he knew not. But, it felt right. In his best reverential voice, he began to intone, "We call upon all Loa, the harvest has ended, and the fields are bare. The earth has grown cold, and the land is empty. The gods of death are lingering over us now. They wait patiently, for eternity is theirs." Moray hesitated, trying to remember the words of the ritual he had witnessed on a number of occasions when he was living, some would say hiding, in Louisiana, exiled from his beloved Virginia. While most of the prayer was remembered, some had to be improvised.

Apallion placed the lantern on the ground a few feet from the supine body. He knelt down beside the boy, Manny, and peeled off his gloves. The dog began to growl in a low rumbling snarl. This would be understandable and a person would want to try to calm the dog, perhaps with a soothing voice, before trying to move it away from the victim. Instead, Apallion's right hand shot out and grabbed the dog by its mottled throat. The canine's yelp was choked off and the dog's eyes went wide in shock. The slightest aura began to build in the dog's eyes and then slowly grew around the captain's hand. His left hand also appeared to grow almost phosphorescent. The glow of the lantern hid this from the others. The light began to fade from the dog's eyes. Apallion's next movement was much subtler. He gently placed his sinister hand on Manny's chest. With an almost disgusted inflection, Apallion growled back at the dog and tossed it aside. It came to rest about six feet from where it had been, never moving after that. The glimmering faded from the confederate's right hand. Manny's body was growing ever so slightly radiant. You would not have seen it from much distance, but if you were up close, it was obvious and otherworldly. Things were changing.

Moray continued on, the prayer now rushing back into his mind. "Hail to you, Aida-Wedo, guardian of the light. When my time comes, I hope you may dream of me worthy. Protect us now. I call...I call upon your power." He emphasized the word, power, with a passion that even impressed him. Perhaps he actually believed in this stuff. "Hail to you, Danbhala-Wedo, for the serpent is reborn. Keep the souls of my ancestors safe within your coils and bless my descendants with your power." Once again, he could not help but shout out the word, power. For all his self-control, Moray was growing almost ecstatic. Surprising even himself, he now remembered most of the words, improvising little. "I call upon the serpent to resurrect this boy. I call upon the rainbow to infuse him with your light. Hail to all Loa who guard the underworld. Accept our sacrifice and return he who is not yet ready to join you. At this time of cold and dark, I honor you with this sacrifice and ask that the rebirth of spring come again. Grant us this wish. Grant us this prayer, and when the day comes that I take my final journey, I will serve you, and you alone." He turned to the father, patted him on the shoulder, and pulled him close. The growing ecstasy that he felt had to be shared. "Now say it with me, Heinrich. Say it for your boy." He nodded at him and squeezed a little tighter. Heinrich Rotz was shaking, overcome with a fear that radiated out from his spine and tormented his muscles. Despite his overwhelming dread, he still joined in on the third word, "...upon all Loa."

Captain Apallion was not listening to them. He knew what had to be done and it was. He evoked the Cajun belief that we all must go to the water when we die. "Nous mourrons tous dans l'eau, c'est vrai. Nous mourrons tous dans l'eau." There was a faint aura remaining near Manny's body when it was done, but it was fading away quickly. After a few more seconds it disappeared completely. Manny's body went rigid. Then he began to shake. Finally, his back arched high into the air and fell back to the ground. The boy became still. Manny looked up and said, "You're the captain."

"I am," was all that Apallion answered.

The boy's hands came up to his chest. He felt all over his torso for the hole he knew should be there, yet it was not. Looking into the captain's eyes, shimmering in the light of the lantern, he said, "You saved me." The captain just nodded. "I pledge my life to you."

"You don't have to. It is already mine for the taking. Now call to your father, Manny." With that Apallion stood up and recovered his lantern. He walked away.

"Daddy?"

With that one vibrant-sounding word, a father's desperation flew from his body. Heinrich looked down at Manny in astonishment. The boy's only motion was to blink his eyes a few times, but it was enough. The man turned to Apallion as he strode past him. "I owe you everything. I owe you my life."

"It's not your life I want." He kept on walking. "Now tend to your boy." Heinrich did not need to be told twice. Manny was starting to rouse a little. Heinrich dropped down, scooped him up, and began hugging him tightly.

Jackson's eyes opened at the same time Manny's did. It was a hard call who was more disoriented. Inside the coffin, Jackson's senses were in complete disarray. It was total darkness, yet he knew his eyes were open. Those same eyes, however, felt like they were going to explode from his head. The pain raced back through his temples and down to the base of his skull. Additionally, there was a throbbing on the right side of his head, and he could feel a gash on his scalp, burning and bleeding. All of the agony was overwhelming his nervous system. Jackson was on the verge of passing out but fought against it with everything he had. He did not know who had attacked him, or how, but he knew he was lucky to wake up from it. There might not be a second time. Too many of his wounded comrades had just wanted to rest a little, just close their eyes for a moment, and they never opened them again. In some ways, the struggle was too much for him. Fighting the pain and trying to regain his senses, allowed fear and anxiety to rise up inside him. All at once both arms shot out but were instantly stymied by the sides of the coffin. The soft, silky lining attached to the sides could not allay his fears. He began to hyperventilate. Quickly, some of his training came back. Jackson latched onto anything he could. In the swirling confusion that was his immediate situation, he began to state, out loud, the steps he took to load his rifle.

There had been times in battle when he would have to talk himself through each step, so the fear would not overtake him. Some of the soldiers he had fought with would load their weapons over and over, without firing. Others would keep pulling the trigger, yet never reload. It was point and click, over and over, until some Yankee piece of lead found them and relieved all of their terror with the answer to "the last question." Some of the men in his platoon thought he was just plum strange, but he never forgot to load or fire his weapon. And he had survived. He had lived to tell the tale. Now, he thought, he would survive again.

As the recitation calmed him, Jackson gathered his thoughts and took back control of his lungs. Ignoring the horrible sounds in his ears and head, he brought his breathing into a relatively normal rhythm. Some of the adrenaline left his bloodstream. With the sudden letdown, his stomach betrayed him. Jackson turned to his right and vomited. The relief that came with emptying his gut would have normally been a good thing. In Jackson's current condition, however, the sudden change in vital signs overwhelmed him. Despite the limited range of movement available, he still felt the world spin a few times. He took a stuttered breath and passed out.

Outside of Jackson's confinement, beside the wagon that held the former Confederate private, Colonel Moray and his chief of staff straightened their uniforms, pulled on their gloves, and made ready to leave with their captured quarry. Then the colonel raised one eyebrow into an arch as he remembered something from earlier. He walked a few steps past his horse, picked up his hat, and dusted it off. With it back on his head, he now felt fully in command of the situation once more. The two men held their heads high and backs straight, confident in the knowledge that they were the raptors of this world. People like Jackson Lee were the prey. Both mounted their horses. Captain Apallion stared beyond the house as if something on the other side had drawn his attention. Colonel Moray surveyed the scene before him. The mission had been successful. There had been casualties, but that is almost unavoidable in this sort of matter. The objective had been accomplished. That was the important thing. Now, he cleared his throat, ready to give one more order to the rabble he was trying to lead. Battles, unfortunately for the people involved, rarely go as planned. The Colonel never had a chance to give that order.

Ψ

"Momma, that horse belongs to the Hubers. It's Selmie's horse."

"Who?" Lenore's response was an honest one. She had no idea

"Anselm. The Hubers."

"What are you talking about, Ellie? How could you know that?"

"I played with him over at the Hubers farm a few times. I even rode him. That's his nicker and whinny. I know it. His name's Glück. Mr. Huber would set us on him and lead us around their farm. Selmie taught me how to talk to him, how to call him." This made Lenore's mind swirl in confusion. She trusted her daughter's senses after so many years of her demonstrating them, but she was not ready for this. She had been kind to the Hubers when few were. Now Walter Huber had come to do them harm? Why? Although they were not close, it was a terrible betrayal nonetheless.

"Why? Why would he...?" Ellie interrupted her questioning with a new turn of events.

"Momma, someone's coming." Lenore immediately began to turn her head toward the two wagon-wheeled tracks that went up past their pond toward the Fairfield Road.

"Where Ellie?" She could not see anyone coming, yet she had grown accustomed to her daughter's impressive sense of hearing. If she heard someone coming, then they were about to arrive. She looked behind them, praying it was not more villainous men. "Where child?" Lenore's nerves were beginning to fray. "Where do you see...where do you hear them at?"

"There's a horse coming up our road." It was then that Lenore heard it too. She had been so spooked that she could not take the time to pray, but if she had, this would have been the answer. Sheriff Streeter went past them on the road about forty yards from the root cellar. His horse was moving beyond a trot. It cantered to the front of the house and stopped just at the limit of where Lenore could still see him. His eyes were clearly focused on the men that Jackson had confronted.

Ψ

George Streeter looked at the situation before him with apparent confusion. Sheriff Streeter was a stoic man, but this was a most unusual occurrence. There was never much trouble in Adams County. Sheriff Streeter had often said to colleagues and friends that he had come along at the right time for this job. After working as a deputy for both Adam Rebert and Phillip Hahn for a total of four years, the people in the county had chosen him to be the next sheriff. The Pennsylvania countryside had remained calm during his tenure. It seemed like someone had determined that after the monstrous violence the area had experienced in the war, it would now know an extended peace. The sheriff had been on his usual, early-morning, six-mile ride from his farm near Fairfield to the office he kept at the county seat, next to the jail. He had seen the fire burning up at the old Hess farm on the small ridgeline north of the road. That would have gotten anyone's attention this early in the morning, but Streeter was not just anyone. It was his job to investigate such things.

Sheriff Streeter shook his head. Ever since the newcomer had bought Hess's farm, there had been concern that something disastrous might happen sooner or later. The lawman had stopped by to meet the man when he had first arrived and welcomed him to Adams County. In reality, his visit was simply meant to survey the mysterious stranger and try to read his intentions. He had found Jackson to be somewhat reticent, if not downright unfriendly, with almost a brooding manner. The only information the law officer had truly gleaned from the meeting was that the new owner of the Hess farm hailed from the western parts of Virginia.

The sheriff had not gone back again but had kept tabs on the man. And there were a lot of tabs to keep. The community, as a whole, had been temporarily scandalized when it became apparent that the newcomer was more than just a neighbor to the widow and her little girl. Sheriff Streeter could not remember the little girl's name as he rode up toward their home. For that matter, he could not remember her mother's name either. It was distracting to him. He should have been thinking about the dangers he might be facing. Instead, he was silently chastising himself for his poor memory and how bad of a neighbor he was, even if he did live several miles down the road. Now, stopping before the house, he finally remembered that they had unique names, Lenore and Electa. Thankfully, for their sake, the gossip about her and the Virginian had dissipated in the light of all the other stories emerging about the man everyone seemed to call Mr. Lee.

The first one was obvious. He was the grandson of the great Confederate general. The story went that he had fallen out with his grandfather over the general's paternalistic compassion for the Negro, and his helping in their education. Others said it had happened earlier, at the end of the war, when he opposed the great general's advocating for the emancipation and enlistment of slaves into the Confederate armies. Like the prodigal son, he had asked for his inheritance and left the Lee family behind in Virginia. When Streeter asked people why he would have come north if he still believed in segregation, people responded that it was one final insult to his grandfather. He would use his inheritance to settle near the place of his grandfather's greatest defeat. It was a tall tale, but entertaining, and obviously false.

Another story that Sheriff Streeter had heard over the summer months was that Mr. Lee was a former Confederate soldier now turned assassin. Ulysses S. Grant had been elected the previous November and inaugurated back in March. Suddenly a new settler comes to the area that's close enough to Washington to be dangerous, yet far enough away to stay out of sight. He was dangerous, this Mr. Lee. What was the good sheriff going to do about it? When Streeter informed them that he intended to do nothing unless the man broke the law, many citizens warned him that by then it would be too late. When another president was gunned down, it would be on his conscience.

The wildest and most bizarre was the final rumor that sprung up around Mr. Lee and his farming. Where had he gotten the money to buy the old Hess farm? If, as Lenore herself had confirmed to friends, Mr. Lee was a former soldier from Dixie, how would he have money? Whether it was invented whole-cloth or based on stories heard during the war, soon enough Mr. Lee was linked to a major train robbery during the summer of '64. It was said that a large shipment of gold bullion had been taken at gunpoint by a band of highly trained Confederate cavalry. Sheriff Streeter tried to explain the logistics of stealing large amounts of gold on horseback. He would go through all the difficulties of defeating a large contingent of soldiers, who were probably experienced in combat, guarding any such shipment. Finally, he would question the propagators of the rumor mill, asking them why the Union army would be moving such a large amount of gold. Did they not know that soldiers were paid in paper currency, never gold? He had heard that many Confederates went months and months without getting paid, or sometimes received scrip instead. However, that did not make for a juicy story to be shared. The images of gold had been fueling many a man's dreams down through the ages. Its enticing luster and color and density would always pull men into crazy schemes to possess it. The men and women of Adams County believed in the conspiracies simply because they were better stories than a mundane one, and the fact that an actual conspiracy had taken away their modern-day prophet, Abraham Lincoln five and half years ago.

Mr. Lee had become a mystery wrapped in another mystery, a gold robbery, which became legend since no one inside or outside the government or military had ever confirmed or denied it. "The General," as Sheriff Streeter referred to the newcomer when talking about him with others, had not helped to quell these stories. The lawman did not believe the rumors making the rounds. Yet, he did think the stranger might have been on the run for some reason. He had vowed to keep an eye on Jackson. So, when the officer of the law turned off the Fairfield Road toward the Hess farm, he thought that trouble had finally caught up with the mystery man. Then he quickly realized that it was currently in progress. There were too many lights and horses and men for anything good to be happening at this time of the morning. The sheriff spurred his horse to move a little faster than its present walking pace. It broke into a canter as Streeter pulled his pistol, a model 1848 Colt Dragoon, from its holster. He did not try to hide his approach. It was best if these men knew he was coming. That way there would be no sudden reactions, no fits of fear that led to gunfire. As he pulled up by the farm's house, he decided to keep the Colt resting gently on his lap. Again, he did not want to spook anyone. It was time to gain control of the situation, but also gather information. The sun was still hidden, so he had to be careful in the light of the torches. Quickly, he surmised that there were nine men in front of him. Some of them looked quite young. A few looked injured.

One of them, Archie, was now in the wagon, ready to take his friend home. The locals had recovered somewhat. Terence stood at his father's side, silently brooding. His brothers stood on the other side. Heinrich had his son on his feet. Though the boy seemed just fine, his father held him tightly, scared that he might fall dead at any moment. For Streeter, it was time to begin assessing how serious this was. The sheriff hailed the party, "Good morning, Gentlemen!" One of the men on horseback had been staring at him already, but now everyone rapidly turned their gaze upon him.

The other man on horseback, a larger fellow, had been speaking, but now turned to the sheriff and said, "And who, sir, might you be?"

The tone of his voice aggravated Streeter. The man thought he was in charge. The sheriff would have to set him straight on that. "I could ask the same of you, sir. My name's George Streeter. I am the sheriff of Adams County." The apparent commander opened his mouth to speak, but Sheriff Streeter did not allow him the privilege. "Now I recognize a number of you men," he barked and then pointed at Moray and Apallion. "But, I don't know you two." He slid his pistol from the middle of his lap onto his right thigh so that it could easily be seen. "I'd be hard pressed to believe all of you were invited by..." He had to pause. He could still not remember the family's surname. "...the widow, Lenore...and her daughter, Electa."

"We have business here with a Mr. Jackson Lee, and it is none of your affair," reported Moray, dismissing the sheriff with a not-so-polite dip of his head.

As the men shuffled about, not sure what their next step should be, the torch light ebbed and flowed. Sheriff Streeter finally got a good look at the two men on horseback. It seemed like they were wearing Confederate uniforms. That rang an alarm in his head. They had to be up to no good. Why else would you put on that uniform? "How'bout you two get down off them horses." The sheriff's eyes quickly looked at the wagon.

He nodded to Archie, "And you get down from there also. The horse had stepped forward two steps, bringing the attention of the sheriff. Archie, the man with the reins, now worked to hold him back. Watching Archie struggle was enough for Streeter to notice the wagon's load. He brought up his Colt while saying, "And I want to know why you have that coffin!"

Ψ

If anyone had been able to gaze upon it, they would have been shocked to see how fast Jackson regained consciousness. He had taken a vicious blow to the head, one that would have killed many people, but Jackson had only been knocked out. With a deep breath, he came back to life once more. However, being awake was one thing, clear in the head was another. The ringing that had been in his ears from the gunshots had been replaced by a distant roaring. Having never been to the coastline, it was the sound Jackson imagined the ocean made as it pounded against a rocky shore. His brain, already addled by the trauma of the blow from the shotgun's stock, became even more confused when Jackson opened his eyes. It seemed like déjà vu to him. He was sure he had seen this emptiness before, but had no memory of waking, even though only a few minutes had gone by since he last passed out.

After a few seconds of letting his eyes adjust, there was still nothing. Everything was black. If he only had his hearing and sight to rely on, Jackson would have concluded that he was dead and leaving our world, passing into the great void. However, he still had some senses remaining. Jackson was thankful for the little things that would have normally been an annoyance. Wherever he was, it smelled bad. It was a musty and decayed smell that seemed somewhat old and fading like it had been a strong stench at one time. Being highly agitated, he was breathing heavy, and every breath tasted dusty, like something had been kicked up into the air when he had been placed here. Finally, he could feel that there were things underneath him that were jabbing into his back, neck, and head. There was no way he had been consigned to oblivion. The great void did not have things poking you in the back. Of this he was certain.

Jackson squeezed his eyes shut, then quickly opened them three times, but still, nothing changed. The blackness was all around him. He moved his head from side to side, feeling the tattered object underneath his head and neck rubbing against his skin. It was a disturbing, but seemingly benign feeling, like when you pick up the shed skin of a snake. Jackson's breathing had slowed a little as some of the renewed adrenaline left his blood. He lifted his right hand to a point in front of his own face. Clenching and opening his fist, Jackson tried to see some movement, but could not. Yet, he was beginning to get a sense of himself and his surroundings. Despite his disorientation, the sickness in the pit of his stomach, and even the roar still pounding in his head, he knew that his hand was in front of him. That was a start, but Jackson also knew he had to see his surroundings before he could begin formulating a plan to get out. Even though he had just thought of the first step in solving the problem, he could not avoid the normal impulse of frustration. Jackson's right leg shot up, and he kicked the lid of the coffin. It did not move at all. He resigned himself to the fact that he was securely imprisoned and moved on to finding a light.

Jackson's thoughts were becoming ever more coherent. He remembered that he had a pack of locofocos in the right front pocket of his pants. Arching his body to the right, he slid his hand down and into the pocket. It was a small relief when his hand found the lucifers. He normally did not bring them to Lenore's home. She did not approve of him rolling an occasional cigarette or enjoying the aroma and flavor of his preferred cigars, so he only did it at his farm. Now, in a lucky turn, he had left the pack of fifty matches in his pants. As he brought the pack up toward his face, he remembered that it was an old pack and there was probably only a handful left. Opening the box took a few seconds of fumbling in the dark, and Jackson felt one of the wooden lucifers fall and hit his chest. It slid off his body to the left. A frown that no one could see came over him. He exhaled in disgust and slowly slid out the piece of sandpaper and another match.

Before he could strike the tip of the match to the paper, Jackson realized that he could hear the muffled sounds of yelling outside his darkened space. He was not moving, for he had felt no acceleration, but something was going on. Even his damaged ears were able to hear it. Perhaps Lenore had gotten Ellie to safety and then found help. If there was help outside his prison, then Jackson was determined to assist in his own emancipation. The noise of the ruckus helped clear Jackson's thoughts even more. The fog that had enshrouded his mind was almost completely lifted, but that doesn't always reveal a bright, sunny day. With clarity of thought came the realization that he was in the wagon, which meant he was in the coffin that had spooked him earlier. Suddenly, Jackson knew what had been poking and rubbing against the back of his head and neck. It sent a shiver through his body, and that revulsion made him drop the sandpaper. He felt it lightly brush against his shoulder as it fell. His sight was useless, but Jackson still knew that the paper had landed atop the body he was lying on. The old demon, panic, began to creep back into his mind.

Yet, his combat experience came through. Once again, he told himself that he had seen the dead, smelled them, and touched their bodies. Twice he had held comrades while they took their last breaths. He was lying on top of a corpse. It was only the remains of someone who had passed on, someone who was gone. It was now just a thing, not an actual being. And that was no reason to panic. It was obvious that Dred had planned this as part of the attempt to break his former subordinate. Jackson's inner counseling worked. Anxiety slipped away, and he began to work on his escape again. First, he needed light. Slowly he began to work his right hand up and back. In the confined space, he struggled to push his hand back and then down far enough to reach the sandpaper. His elbow pushed into the lid of the casket. Pain began to build in his shoulder and elbow as he tried to force his hand down without knocking the sandpaper farther beyond his reach. For several moments his hand could not move any deeper.

In a moment of insight, Jackson realized he could swing his hand back and forth in the hopes of finding the sandpaper, but he had to be ever so careful. The paper could easily get lost in the decaying clothes and body of the corpse underneath him. Gently he moved his hand in toward his neck. It was at the limit of his flexibility that he found the most surprising thing; metal, cool and delicate metal. The tactile sensation quickly became the conclusion that it was a small chain, clearly a necklace. For some reason, some purpose he could not explain, Jackson wanted to grab hold of the chain and take it. He ran two fingertips over the carved lines and crevices of the pendant. A light came on in his eyes but was extinguished just as fast. There was something there that he wanted. It was as fleeting as a drunken memory. He could not make the connection. His mind and fingers broke away from the necklace. He slid his fingers along the collarbone of the corpse very slowly. There was a sudden stop where the clavicle met the shoulder. He pulled his hand back reflexively. With even more care he moved again and was rewarded. The paper was there. With the skill of a surgeon, he lifted his fingers up and came down on top of it, knowing that an attempt from the side could push it off the corpse's shoulder.

The process was reversed until Jackson had his hands at his sides and the sandpaper and lucifers held firmly. Yet, he did not create light. He remained motionless, staring into the darkness. Something was gnawing at the back of his mind, and it was not the teeth from the leathery skull underneath him. He had to have that necklace. It was not that Jackson wanted to become a grave robber. He simply needed to look at it, study it, and feel the pendant's shape and texture. The thought that he kept coming back to was that he had to hold it once more. He must hold it. It did not make sense to him, but it was overwhelming nonetheless. The pendant needed to be in his hands. The sandpaper and lucifers went into his pockets. Knowing how to move his arm from the retrieval of the match made the second attempt much more proficient. Little time had passed before Jackson had the necklace in his hand. Now came a terrible thought. He realized that there was no way for him to release the necklace properly. He had to break the chain. Now that horrible thought was lodged in his mind. If he pulled on the pendant with too much force and the chain was made of a sturdy metal, it might rip through the decayed flesh and bone of the corpse, severing its head. Though he knew the body beneath him was no longer a human being, Jackson was not about to desecrate the corpse like that. Yet, the fact remained; he had to see and hold that necklace. He considered his options, a slow pull versus a quick yank. Then he decided on a plan.

Slowly he pushed his head back against the body underneath him. He felt the desiccated face push back against his hair and rub against his neck. Jackson grimaced but held firm. With as much force as he could generate in the confined space, he yanked the pendant back instead of up, hoping to use the skull as a focal point, avoiding the neck. It worked and with a snap the necklace was free. Jackson shifted the piece of jewelry to his chest, laying it in a spot where he knew it would not slide away. With care and precision, he then reached into his pockets and retrieved the lucifers and the striking paper. He brought the wooden match's phosphorus tip to the edge of the sandpaper, took a deep breath, and struck. A few sparks flew, but nothing came of it. He breathed in deeply and repeated the process. Suddenly, the lucifer shot out several sparks, stuttered, and then blazed to life. The expected, yet swift, appearance of light in the small space hurt his eyes momentarily. He blinked a few times then shut his eyes. Quickly, he realized the futility of that action, understanding that time was limited when it came to the small locofoco. He opened his eyes again, lifted the necklace to the match, and stared at an exquisitely carved representation of his ancestor. Her lovely, carved face connected him to his Bams, which led him to Annabel, and that brought him back to...the coffin.

"Nooooooo!" Jackson's legs started kicking. The match dropped and he began punching the lid of the casket. "You son of a bitch, Moray! You goddamn bastard!" The cameo was clenched tight in his one hand, but the other three limbs were striking out as best they could in the cramped space. "I'll kill you, you bastard! I'll kill you!" The match he had dropped had not gone out. It fell against the bottom of the coffin and immediately ignited the lining of it. The inside of the casket was beginning to burn. Jackson did not notice. He screamed at Moray. Archie, once a friend, was now a treacherous enemy. And of course, Old Scratch, Captain Apallion, received his venomous accusations as well. "I'll kill every one of you. You're dead, Huber! You and all your sons are dead!" Normally, a man's rage will burn itself out. Jackson's was simply growing. His fist drove upward in an uppercut motion and smashed into the lid of the coffin again, but this time the knuckle on his middle finger fractured. He did not feel it. A few seconds later, the old boot on his left foot gave way, tearing away from the sole. With the next kick, Jackson broke his big toe. Nothing registered. He continued screaming invective. All of his efforts had done nothing to free him, but it did accomplish something.

Caibideil a Còig

...because no matter where you're heading,

there you are.

"My God, is there a man in there?" asked Sheriff Streeter. He knew the answer to the question before he even uttered the words. "That man's alive!" It was shocking to him, but something everyone else already knew. Nobody reacted to the statement. Nobody moved. "You there," he shouted to Archie. "Get that man out of that coffin!" He let go of the reins and his horse immediately turned a bit to the left. In keeping everyone in his sights he had to twist a little to the right. It brought the Colt up for balance, pointing in the direction of Jackson's former comrade. After all that had just happened, the sight of one more gun did not alarm anyone. Yet, it triggered something far worse than fear.

"Not again!" yelled Archie as he stood up from the wagon's bench seat. There was a rifle to his right, held in a scabbard tied to the seat. As the former soldier reached for the weapon, he hollered, "You beat me here once. I won't have it again!" He pulled the rifle out and pulled the hammer back as he turned toward Streeter.

"No more!" he roared right before the weapon did. The projectile was on target, heading straight for the lawman's chest. Sheriff Streeter surely would have been killed then and there if not for the peaceful life his horse had led up to that point in time. He was riding a draft horse this morning instead of his normal Appaloosa, which was lame with an infection in tis hoof. The draft horse reacted poorly to the hollering long before the shot rang out. He spun a little to the right just as Archie fired. The bullet missed Streeter, creased the horse's neck, and kept on traveling, coming to rest near the Fairfield Road.

Lenore jumped at the sound of the rifle and pushed Ellie down behind the wall. Ellie squirmed away from her and rose back up. "What's happening?" Lenore could only see the sheriff. She really did not know what was happening but understood it was bad. In the confusion, a brief moment of clarity opened up to her. A moment earlier Lenore had not even realized the sheriff's words had reached her ears and then her brain. Now what the sheriff had said about a man being in a coffin was suddenly transparent. Jackson, her Jacks, was locked up in a coffin. What could possibly be happening in front of her house? It seemed as though an unexpected maelstrom of madness had engulfed them all.

Streeter immediately pulled the reins back to the left, stabilized the horse, and let loose with a round from his Colt. It was simply meant to return fire and keep the man with the rifle pinned down. There was no way he thought it would end the exchange. He was moving on the horse. The pistol was moving as he brought it up and fired. Even Archie was moving as he lowered his weapon to see if his shot had struck home. There are times, however, when everything comes together and you make a lucky shot. Though Archie's luck had run out.

The Hubers did not take the time to label it as anything other than one shot too many. They had reached their threshold of gun violence. All four of them began to run toward the pond, hoping to get to the Fairfield Road while avoiding the sheriff, who was blocking the way. Heinrich Rotz half-pulled and half-carried his son, Manny, toward the far end of the farmhouse. This night, and this entire plan, had been a huge Rotz, as they made it to the corner of the house. At least it would be over soon, for him and his son. That's what he kept repeating in his mind. This would all be over soon. He was wrong, of course. Young Herman Rotz called out for his German short-hair as they fled, but the dog never moved. Its lifeless eyes stared blankly in the direction of the wagon that, for the moment, still held both Archie and Jackson.

A look of pure shock came over Archie's face as he felt the collision of the sheriff's bullet with his chest and realized he had lost again. The impact drove him straight back into the seat of the wagon and forced him to drop the rifle. His chin dropped toward his chest, and he stared at the hole in his uniform. Images of his life did not enter his mind. There were no memories of his lost family or the lost cause. He simply wondered how long he had to live. The former soldier looked back at the lawman with the large pistol and said, "Had to be. I was never meant to escape Gettys..." An interrupted life ended with a fall, not from grace, but from the bench of an old teamster's wagon.

Archie's body landed on the ground to the right of the four-wheeled farm cart. Supine, he looked as if he had lied down in the grass for a short nap or to stare up at the stars that were now dimming in the coming light of morning. The horse that had drawn the wagon to this fateful moment began to rise up on its hind legs. It continued rearing but never moved forward. The other horses, which had so recently been collected, became agitated as well, but they were not hitched to a wagon. Rider or not, they knew it was time to leave. Everything was turning to chaos. Everything was in motion.

Colonel Moray was moving before Archie had hit the seat. He spurred his horse while pulling the reins. The colonel's horse drew close to Captain Apallion's. With a swipe of his hand, Moray grabbed the lantern from his chief of staff's grip and howled, "Ride, Captain! Ride!" Apallion immediately followed the order. He drew his reins to the right and began to circle around the back of the wagon. In a few steps of his horse, Apallion had his pistol out and in his left hand. Sheriff Streeter was not looking at him, however. His gaze was fixated on the tall man holding up the lantern and shouting, "I will meet you at the ferry where this all began!" Streeter's horse spun back to the right again as Moray said in a much lower voice, "But, first, I will take care of Private Lee."

Apallion heard him but did not answer. He was focused on the sheriff, whose back was now turned to the fleeing Confederate officer. There was no question as to what Apallion would do. Sometimes Moray could be a pompous fool, but for Apallion, he was a useful fool, and he deserved loyalty and protection. Three shots erupted from the captain's pistol, a Lefaucheux M1858. The first and the last missed badly, but the second one hit home. It shattered Streeter's sixth rib on the right side, front and back, as the bullet tore into and exited his body.

At the same moment, Moray brought his horse next to the Huber's wagon. A brief moment of memory came to him as he thought of Huber's reluctance a few days ago when he picked up the package from South Carolina at the train station. Moray had played them all, convincing officials in Charleston that his former comrade in arms, Jackson Lee, had wanted more than anything for his beloved wife to be buried on his new farm in Pennsylvania. It was all part of the healing of the nation. The officials understood that even better after a few gold pieces were carelessly left on their desks by Captain Apallion. One gold piece was enough for Huber's reluctance to be practically overwhelmed. Gold; it is a beautiful thing. That was all that Moray now thought as he smashed the kerosene lantern onto the coffin's lid. The flammable liquid spread across the wood and quickly ignited. Moray, reacting to the movement of Glück's constant rearing and the shots fired by his subordinate, now pulled his pistol and made ready for battle. No immediate fight was coming. Sheriff Streeter had fallen from his mount.

When Apallion's bullet found its mark, the lawman was twisted out of his saddle by the momentum of the large piece of lead. However, the saddle, or more precisely the stirrups, had not let go completely. Streeter's boot was caught, holding his right leg high off the ground as he lay on it. He might have been dragged away if the old draft horse had not been so confused by the thunder of guns and the shrill shouting of men drawn into a mêlée. Frenchie simply kept spinning to the right and then back to his left, rolling the sheriff over, dragging him, and punishing his body to the point of it going into shock. The real danger, however, came from his hooves. Streeter brought his arms up over his face and head, trying to protect himself while still being able to see and avoid the horse's stomping. There was a piercing pain from his side that was becoming unbearable, but he had to stay conscious. If he lost that fight, he was going to lose it all. He knew that one shot from his massive steed's shod hooves would probably mean the end for him. Fighting against the pulls and twists of the horse was all he could manage. There was no time to get his boot unstuck, or even off.

Moray next looked around for the other men he had brought with him. Only Archie could be seen, but he was dead, frozen in his final act of rebellion. The rest had fled the fracas. Jackson Lee, the simple private his officers had teased by calling him "General," was all that remained. Through the growing flames, Moray could hear the muffled shouts of his quarry. It sounded painful. That would have to be the one pleasure he got from his final foray into the north. He now realized that it had been a mistake to come here once again, but from the moment Captain Apallion had first raised the idea of gathering together his old forces, Moray had insisted on collecting the deserters before any others. Now

Galloway was dead, and Lee soon would be. Such was the way of warfare. They would begin again. This time they would search for Sergeant John McClintock, and his legendary gold. Yet, before quitting the field, he wanted to watch Lee burn a little more. It was a tactical mistake on the part of Moray. Once you decide to retreat then you must commit to it. Waiting only opens you up to more attacks.

Inside the coffin, Jackson had still not come to understand that his defiant screaming and pounding were to no avail. His throat was now raw, the same as his nerves. Too far gone into the madness and terror, he could not even notice that the slow fire burning through the lining of the coffin was starting to ignite his own clothes. For the moment, he did not feel the heat. Nor did he recognize the pain. All that remained within his focus was the horror that he felt. Not even an hour before this, he had been confronting the death of his wife for the first time. Now he was lying on top of her dead and decaying body. His bones were broken. His hands and toes were covered in blood. His arms and legs were being burned. And all he wanted was to get hold of Colonel Hildred Moray's throat. No, that was not it. The thing he wanted most of all was to lay Annabel to rest again. She did not deserve this obscenity. Then, and only then, would he kill Moray. Yet, before all that, he had to get out of this casket he was trapped in. The only fortunate thing for Jackson was the limited oxygen supply as the air had trouble seeping through the small spaces in the coffin, which was not air-tight. It kept the fire from blazing bright, but now it also worked against him. The smoke had nowhere to go, and the oxygen inside his tiny prison was almost used up. Jackson began to cough violently.

There was no conscious choice, but somewhere in this moment, his mind switched to survival. He stopped trying to escape his confinement and began to pound on the lining to put out the remaining flames. Now his hands were burned in addition to being broken and bloodied. Once the flames were extinguished, something new became clear. There was still tremendous heat within his confined space and incredibly small lines of light filtered inside the wood walls and through the smoke. The coffin, Jackson quickly realized, was also burning on the outside. The man who had survived so much was finally succumbing. He became dizzy once more. He coughed again and again. Breathing was growing difficult. The world was quickly slipping away. Perhaps this time would be the last.

Lenore could not see any of the struggles her Jacks was going through or the look of gleeful satisfaction on Colonel Moray's face. All she saw was that the man who had ridden in to save the day was now in danger of being trampled by his own horse. A helpless human being always spurred her to action, and this was no different. She grabbed hold of Ellie by the arms, picked her up and placed her in the root cellar. "Stay here, child. I have to help the sheriff," was all she said before closing the door. It did not stay shut for even the briefest amount of time. As Lenore ran up from the root cellar door and into the whirlwind of battle, her daughter was intent on one thing, saving Mr. Jacks. Like mother like daughter, Lenore ran toward the sheriff while Ellie came up to the stone retaining wall that led into the cellar. The mother had dealt with horses and before she had closed within forty feet of the sheriff she began talking to the horse in a commanding yet friendly way. "Whoa, big boy! Whoa! Come now. I have you! I have you!" She closed the distance quickly. The amount of circumference in the horse's spin began to get smaller and smaller. Lenore was so focused on Streeter's stallion that she did not notice the sound her daughter made. Colonel Moray did.

Ψ

A shrill whistle erupted from behind the farmhouse. It was two quick bursts followed by a rising and falling siren. The Huber's draft horse stopped rearing, became still, and pricked its ears up. Moray's head snapped toward the house. His eyes glared into the night, but he was baffled by what he saw. A woman, probably the owner of this farm, the one Rotz had called a nigger-loving whore, was running toward the peacekeeper who was about to be stomped into oblivion, and the ground. It was obvious that the call could not have come from her. Quickly he knew that she was talking to the horse, not whistling at it. Then the call came again, and Moray could not believe what he saw. The old horse strained against the harness and began to pull the fiery wagon toward the house. Was it Huber? No. They had fled in the opposite direction. What could possibly be going wrong now? Moray knew he should flee. A retreat had been called for, but would this new development snatch his small victory away from him? For the first time since his exile to Louisiana, Moray was wracked with indecisiveness.

Ψ

Lenore was not. She approached Streeter and his steed rapidly but knew not to get close enough to be kicked. Both arms were outstretched and raised, trying to convey as large an image as possible. "Look at me, boy! Look at me." Old Frenchie did just that, while still rearing halfway. Lenore instinctively stepped back two steps. Still, she kept talking. "Be calm, boy! Just be calm. Whoa. Whoa, now. Nobody is going to hurt you." Her voice was dropping in intensity. "Nobody is going to hurt you." Frenchie became still.

Herr Glück did not. The cart was rolling, and he was being called by his master. One more time the whistle came. Glück snorted loudly and then whinnied, trying to answer the call. Ellie heard his answer and yelled back, "This way, Glück! Here I am!" A crazy, but important, thought came to her. From memory and feel she ducked into the cellar, reached into the potato bin, and grabbed two of them before reemerging into the dawning light. Ellie heard him coming up to the root cellar and let loose with three high-pitched whistles. The horse immediately brought the wagon to a stop. Ellie rushed up to meet him. She felt for his nose, focusing on a snort and heavy breathing. The potatoes were quickly offered and Glück enjoyed them, but the little girl could hear and feel that he was still highly agitated. And though she could not see it, she could also hear and feel, as she moved down the hitch and harness toward the wagon, that it was on fire. "Mr. Jacks! Mr. Jacks!" she cried out as she began to feel for a step. Her hands quickly found it, and then she climbed up into the wagon.

Ψ

Moray had watched his former soldier going up in flames. Then he just watched him go. The officer was frozen by the absurdity of it all. Without anyone at the reins, the wagon and its grotesque cargo, just left. There was more than a moment of disbelief before the officer regained his composure. Then he spurred his horse and went after the escaping wagon. Time was growing short. Everything before his eyes seemed condensed.

Ψ

Lenore was moving in the opposite direction, slowly approaching the side of Sheriff Streeter's mount. She was so focused on saving the sheriff that she had not noticed the wagon go past her. In an instant, she pulled the lawman's foot out of his boot. Next, she got her arms under his and began to drag him away from the horse. He cried out in pain for a short beat, but then stifled his shriek, trying to maintain his dignity. It did not last. With her exertion, Lenore was not so single-minded and did see the flash of a different horse explode past her as Moray chased the wagon. Instinctively knowing that danger was heading for her daughter, Lenore dropped the sheriff and turned toward Ellie and the root cellar. Another yelp of pain was heard by Lenore as Streeter landed on his broken rib. Yet, she was not looking back. Neither was Moray. It was only a few strides and he had caught up to the buckboard. Amazingly, he was stunned into momentary disbelief and paralysis again. For if he had been given a million chances, he could never have predicted this night would produce the scene in front of him.

Ellie had initially climbed up onto the seat. "Mr. Jacks, are you there? Where are you, Mr. Jacks?" The flames had caught the side of the wagon nearest the house on fire. The conflagration was spreading. Jackson could no longer answer, or help in any possible way. The lack of oxygen had returned the man to a state of unconsciousness. The little girl, who had come to love the former soldier, a soldier who had returned to being a farmer during the past year, imagined herself as a hero like she envisioned Mr. Jacks being. She did not feel any fear. There was only an overwhelming drive to help. In a few seconds, she had stripped off her warm jacket, jumped over the seat, and, with her coat, began pounding on the box she had heard someone say Mr. Jacks was in. She was slapping at the flames and actually making progress in smothering them on the end of the coffin near the front of the wagon. "Mr. Jacks, it's Miss Electa! I'm here, Mr. Jacks!"

Ψ

Her worried cry broke Moray from his second spell of incredulity. "You there, get down from the wagon! Get away from there!" he screamed at the little girl. The child was not one of his soldiers, not a pawn on a chessboard. Ellie heard the voice, recognized it from earlier, and then dutifully ignored him. She was not ruled by political machinations or arguments of good and evil or even honor. All she knew was that Mr. Jacks had to be saved.

Any sense of control was now gone from the Confederate commander. This final insult was too much. What little triumph he had achieved here in Pennsylvania was now to be undone by some child in a nightgown who seemed to be blindly smothering Private Lee's flames of damnation with a wretched, little smock. He would not stand for it. The elitist chivalry that had been instilled in him by his father, teachers, and antebellum superiors, drove him during the war and maintained him in exile, disappeared in the rising smoke of the wagon. He brought his pistol to bear on a little girl. A murderous glare came over his eyes. "Damn you, you child of perdition! I said get away from there!" Ellie looked in the direction of the ranting madman, but her unseeing eyes could betray no fear. Whether he would have actually pulled the trigger would never be answered. Ellie heard the thud of something solid and heavy hitting bone.

Moray felt the impact of the smooth projectile as it concussed his head. His sight left him for just a second. In that moment of blindness, a strange thought came to him. A wave of internal anger and fury focused on something trivial, but it is usually a little detail that sends a man over the edge. He could not believe that he had lost his hat for a second time. "No! No! No!" was all he could muster. His free hand came up to his head, and he felt a large lump already beginning to rise on his skull. A few squints of his eyes and his sight returned just in time to see a second Mason jar hurling his way. He reflexively fired off a shot and got lucky for the moment. The Mason jar exploded right before it hit him, but glass and alcohol sprayed all over his uniform and the head of his charger. He turned to look at the horse but realized he had made a mistake and quickly turned back. It was in time to see the final Mason jar coming at him in a shallow arc. Moray only had time to swing his pistol. It hit the glass jar, shattering it into tiny shards. Much of the moonshine rained down on his saddle and the hindquarters of his horse. Now his attention turned to the source of the attack. Beyond the buckboard, standing by some type of half-buried building, was a woman. This was who had accosted him with jars of whiskey. The indignity seemed to never end. Moray aimed his pistol and fired just behind the Huber's horse. Remarkably, the draught animal remained calm, still enjoying the last of the potatoes. The shot missed, and Lenore jumped over the retaining wall of the entrance to the cellar. She reached inside and pulled out the lantern she had left behind minutes earlier. Moray directed his horse to the left and came clear of the beast of burden attached to the burning buckboard. He now looked directly at Lenore.

"You are the Whore of Babylon so many spoke of." One final time Moray's gloved hand brought up his cherished pistol. It was from the London Armoury Company and he had purchased it in 1857 on his one trip abroad. The sight on the front of the barrel was aligned with Lenore's chest. "You are an abomination!" growled Moray. There was no escape, but nothing in the world is one hundred percent certain. Moray decided to shoot the woman in the head just as Ellie screamed for Lenore. For the briefest of moments, the colonel looked in the direction of the little girl. The distraction caused by the child, made his decision to change his aiming point a fatal mistake. As the gun roared to life, Lenore ducked instinctively, but the bullet had already passed her head, missing by at least half a foot.

"No, I am a mother!" shouted Lenore as she heaved the lantern at the monstrous man on horseback. The lamp missed him, but sometimes pinpoint accuracy does not matter. The lantern connected in a loud crash with the stock of Moray's rifle, which was sticking out of the scabbard behind his fine English saddle. It had the same effect as the lantern he had thrown down on Annabel's coffin, only doubly so due to the alcohol vapors enveloping him. The South would not rise again, under Moray's leadership or anyone else's. An inferno blazed to life. The lantern's once controlled flame was now free.

There was an instant hellfire. The top of the horse was burning, from its tail to its mane. Moray was completely engulfed in blue, orange, and yellow light. The heat was excruciating as his neatly trimmed hair and beard were singed and his skin crackled. The echoes of his screaming, "Aaaaaaaaahhhhhhhh!" split the night as Moray and his horse raced in the direction of what he considered to be the true netherworld, the north. He was never seen again.

Ψ

Lenore could only watch him go for a couple of seconds. The battle was now over, but the struggle was not. Ellie had continued to strike out at the heat she felt and the crackling she heard with her now scorched coat as fast she could. She had been so brave. She had fought so hard, but her limited number of years meant there was little endurance. Fatigue was taking over, and the flames burned higher. Lenore turned back to her daughter, who was desperately trying to save Jackson, but to her mother only seemed to put herself in mortal danger. With a swiftness she never wanted to know again, because it was fueled by so much fear, Lenore was at the wagon and demanded, "Ellie get down from there before you're killed!"

The daughter was stubborn because she usually got her way, but also because she knew that Jackson was there. Even though she had not heard his voice once since she climbed onto the wagon, Ellie simply knew that he was there. "No, Momma! It's Mr. Jacks!" Lenore was quickly up on the wagon's seat. She reached out and grabbed hold of Ellie. Immediately, the girl wrestled away from her grip. "No, Momma!" Lenore needed to move quickly. She reached out farther, but as she did, her knee brushed against a thick, folded, wool blanket that had almost been pushed off the seat by all of the scuffling. It was the catalyst that changed her direction. She picked it up and clambered over the seat and into the bed of the wagon. Now she too fought the flames. It was far more effective than her daughter, but that would never diminish the courageous effort that would be told by all of Ellie's descendants.

Yet, as hard as the two of them fought, they could not defeat the fire. If they were going to save Jackson, something else had to be done. It was then that Lenore noticed something about Huber's horse-drawn truck. It was a stake body and it looked like the slats could be removed. An idea came to her, but it held little hope. "Get back, Ellie," ordered Lenore as she dropped the blanket and picked up her daughter.

"No. No! I need to…"

"I need room," shouted Lenore as she moved Ellie back to the seat. She looked her daughter in the eye and then shook her head, irritated with herself. After all these years, she still wanted to communicate with Ellie visually. Even without it, the girl seemed to understand and stopped fighting. Lenore promptly got to work. She pulled out the first of the wagon's slats on the side of the root cellar. It was very heavy for her, but she only had to lift it a small amount and then let it fall to the ground. The second slat would not budge; one pull, two pulls, three, and nothing. Then on the fourth, she yelled, "Come on!" and it moved. It took a fifth pull and it was free. Yet, the fire had regained ground. It covered the coffin once more. Still, Lenore was not defeated. She went to the back of the wagon and stepped toward the corner of the casket, but the flames beat her back. She kicked at the wooden container, but it moved only a small distance. It felt like it weighed five hundred pounds. It did not matter.

Lenore was now reaching the point of white rage. The whirlwind had taken her too. Over and over again she kicked at the back corner until the coffin was near the edge of the bed. She picked up her nightgown jumped down to the ground, and then just as quickly scrambled up into the front of the bed. Once there she repeatedly kicked and kicked and kicked with all she had. Ellie, wanting to help but not knowing how began to swing her coat at the casket again. It did not distract Lenore from her ultimate goal. The coffin edged closer and closer to the tipping point.

As if accusing the red-streaked sky of being complicit, Lenore hollered, "I want this to end now!" and she gave the burning box one final thrust with her boot. The casket teetered slightly and then as if Jackson had rolled with it, the final resting place of Annabel Lee came crashing to the ground. It was not a tremendous fall, but the coffin had rotated as it fell. It hit on the corner of the lid and the sidewall of the shell. The collision had enough force to tear off the hastily added clasp that had trapped Jackson in the coffin. It rolled over and spun out Jackson, and something that terrified Lenore. Gazing upon the decayed remains in the light of the burning wagon made her scream.

Her terror elicited a "Momma!" from her daughter, which refocused Lenore before the sound of Ellie's voice had dissipated. She got her daughter down from the wagon and carried her away from the fire and the now opened casket. "Stay right here." Lenore turned back to the coffin, but just as quickly spun back around. "I mean it, Ellie. Don't move!"

The willfulness displayed earlier had drained away. Like many people, Ellie was starting to feel the danger she had been in only now that it had passed. "I won't Momma. I won't. I'll stay right here." Lenore turned away again and hurried to Jackson's side.

"Jacks! Jacks! Speak to me, Jackson." He was not talking. With a strength that came partly from being a woman who ran a farm by herself and partly from a not yet dissipated fear, Lenore reached underneath Jackson's arms and began to slide him away from the wagon and the relatively ornate sarcophagus. "Come on, Jacks! Wake up, Honey. Wake up!" She continued to slowly slide him along the ground until they had come to Ellie. The little girl had kept her promise, not moving hardly a muscle, listening intently to her mother struggle with Jackson's long body. Upon reaching Ellie's side, she stopped. After a moment's pause, she took one more step and fell backward, collapsing into a seated position. It was not planned, but Jackson fell perfectly with his head resting on one of her legs. Lenore leaned forward and took his head in her hands. Gently, she turned his face to hers. Ellie knelt beside her, reached out, and stroked

Jackson's hair. "Come back to us now, Jacks. You know I said, 'Yes.'" Her daughter looked up with a curious look on her face, but her mother did not stop to explain. "I said, 'Yes,' Jacks." She envisioned him opening his eyes and smiling at her, saying, "Sure, Lenore, I remember now." Yet, he remained motionless. "Please, Jacks." Tears began to spill out of her eyes and run down her cheeks. One teardrop fell from Lenore onto Jackson's nose, and then it happened. Her soldier, her champion, erupted into a coughing fit. It was short-lived, but afterward, Jackson was breathing easier and stronger. Though not the romantic moment she had pictured, it was enough.

Lenore looked to the East and saw the risen sun, and she knew that they had won. She continued to hold Jackson's head, but also pulled Ellie tight to her chest and began to weep. The sun continued to rise over the horizon. Night had ended. Now that Jackson had shown some sparks of life, all Lenore could think of was how close she had come to losing Ellie. She loved Jackson. Her words had been true, and she wanted to marry him now more than ever, but the only thoughts in her head at this moment were of her daughter. There was an overwhelming feeling of love and fear mixed together. It was the two emotions that ran high in every parent. With her chest convulsing and jaw shaking, she looked to the sun again, took a deep breath, and accepted that they were safe. It now came to her that before she could go get help from her closest neighbors; she had to get Jackson and Sheriff Streeter inside the house. Glück had gotten worked up again, understandably so. He had slowly pulled the blazing wagon away. He would need to be released soon before the fire grew too large and burned him. There was so much to do.   Lenore released Ellie, gently laid Jackson's head on the ground, and wearily stood up. A woman's work was never done.

Chapter Fifteen

...because every story must have a place where it starts.

"Jack, do you really have to cover my eyes?" He nudged Hannah a little to prompt her to go in the right direction.

"Of course you do. I want this to be a surprise."

"You're being so suspicious," declared Hannah. "First you blindfold me all the way out here. Now the blindfold is not good enough. You have to cover my eyes with your hands."

"Do you remember the second time we ever met?" They continued walking and talking like this, as if it was as natural as a butterfly darting through a meadow.

"Of course, you had set a trap for me. Tempting me with fresh bread and grape jelly, sitting on a lovely blanket I assume belonged to your aunt. You were waiting there by the stream when you should have been working."

"Wow! I see you really do remember it well." Hannah stopped walking for a moment.

"You really like that new word I told you about. You use it all the time."

"What? Wow? I must admit, I do like it," agreed Jack. "It has a force to it. You know, it's just that you surprised me with all of those details."

"How could I forget? It's the first time you ever kissed me."

"I kissed you? Are you...All right. All right. My point is, you covered my eyes with your hands then."

"Yes, I did." Hannah smiled at the memory of her teasing.

"And from that moment, good things have happened. I just really want this to go well, my love. So, if you will bear with me a few more steps." They proceeded to carefully take those last few paces. "Hannah, I present to you...Lóchrann Manor!" He immediately removed his hands and Hannah opened her eyes.

An empty house lay before her. There was a fence of carefully stacked field stone between her and the home. She looked to the wooden gate. It needed whitewashed. Her eyes moved to the front of the house. It was small, with four rectangle windows and a small square window above the door. Two large chimneys stood on either side of the house, indicating that rooms on either side most likely contained fireplaces. Hannah narrowed her focus and looked to the entrance. The door's knocker was ready to fall off. Next, she looked to the roof. It was slate, and there were many broken shingles. Yet, the roof shocked her more than anything because she knew what Jack calling the place Lóchrann Manor meant. This was to be their home. "How could you afford this, Jack?"

"What do you mean?" he begged.

"Well, I don't belong to any guild, but I am not so ignorant that I don't know it costs a pretty penny to have a slater put on a roof such as that."

"That's true, but if you look carefully, you will see that it was not very well maintained."

"Wait. I know where I am at now. This is the old Smithson place."

"That's right. It was part of the Percy Estate. I think it was a guest house or something like that. History lesson, my dear; they broke up the estate years ago. This became the Smithson farm. See the barn back there?" She looked where he was pointing.

"That's a barn?" she asked without considering the impoliteness of her question. Fortunately, Jack was too excited to notice.

"It's a little small, but it's got everything I need for our livestock, at least for now." Hannah looked around carefully and then kissed him fully. They were not yet married, and she did not want any scandal for Jack.

"I am so proud of you. You've worked so hard. And you save almost everything, never taking pleasure in the fruits of your labor." He looked down as his face became a bit flushed.

"Well, I still did not have enough to buy this farm."

"Then how did you acquire…"

Jack interrupted her question. "I asked my uncle."

"Oh, Jack. You did not have to do that." She knew that Jack's relationship had never improved much beyond Master and hired hand. He had never come to look at his nephew as more than an individual whom he had helped once. That one moment of assistance to Jack, or in truth, to his parents, seemed to breed a measure of resentment in his uncle that Jack could never overcome. Turning to his aunt would have been useless. She was wholly subservient to her husband.

"It's all right. We will make this the finest farm in the county, maybe in all the shires around us too."

Hannah continued her subtle objection. "But you said you didn't want to take anything from your uncle."

"I made him a business proposition. He was not going to give me anything, even if I groveled on my knees before his beloved writing table, for he doesn't believe in usury. Just spouts off a bunch of verses from Saints Matthew and Luke."

"He should try 'Give to the one who asks you, and do not turn away from the one who wants to borrow from you.' Matthew 5:42."

"How do you know that?" asked Jack in wonderment.

"It's just an opinion, Jack. I simply meant that your uncle might..."

He stopped her with an emphatic, "No." Then he softened his voice and said, "No. I'm sure you're right about that, but how do you recite such things?"

"I love to read the scriptures. You know that I do. You should too." Jack shook his head to demonstrate his lack of comprehension and that he would not be joining her any time soon.

Instead, his amazement continued unabated. "Yes, but how do you remember it all?"

"It takes a lot of work," answered Hannah without a hint of hesitation.

"Well, I am pretty sure my uncle threw that one at me too. To be honest, I stopped listening to him more than a year ago. But, back to how I got the money. He made an investment in us, and that is about as compassionate as he can be. For a certain percentage of any profits the farm will have over the next ten years, he was willing to make up the rest that I needed."

"So, this is ours?" Though Jack had discovered a long time ago that he was not Hannah's intellectual equal, he still enjoyed playing with her mind, if only to see her response.

"Well, that depends. You still have to go through with marrying me. Perhaps I should get the notary and draw up a contract."

"Stop it!" she demanded. "You will not turn into your uncle. And you will not be needing a notarized contract. I am with you through good and bad, my dearest."

"It is your love that drives me." He smiled and kissed her again without looking to see if anyone was around. "I do love you, my darling."

"And I love Lóchrann Manor. Although, that name is so terribly pretentious."

"Well, I meant it as a joke, but the joke is on me because I am now starting to like the sound of it. I guess I must be a little pretentious."

"Will I have to start calling you Lord Lóchrann?" asked Hannah.

"Let's just stick with Jack. Or you can address me as the dearest, sweetest, most handsome man in all of England," he said loudly while raising his one hand as if addressing all the vines and wildflowers that had grown over the stone fence. "For I would much prefer that those words be uttered by your divinely red lips."

"I am going to go with Lord Lóchrann then."

"Oh, if you insist." Jack was trying to give his best impression of a gentleman from the aristocracy. It was not a very good one. He had no contact with any aristocrats. Even his uncle, despite acquiring a large amount of wealth, was still considered a yeoman farmer. That was what Jack aspired to. "Then come along Lady Lóchrann. Let me show you where you will soon be living in the luxury of our humble estate." They walked to the gate. Jack put one hand on the top of it and gave a gentle push. It promptly fell off the post, taking the hinges with it.

Chapter Six

...because there are six strings and they reveal the universe.

Jackson opened his eyes and knew that it had all been a dream. Of that, he was certain. Why else would he be looking directly at the ceiling of his own home. It was easily recognizable, what with the stains from the water that had begun leaking in when the rains of autumn had started a month ago. It was one of those tasks you keep telling yourself that you will fix just as soon as the present crisis passes, but you never do. A bucket is placed. The rain stops. Other problems arise to be focused on. A dripping ceiling is not going to kill someone. With that last thought, all of the details of the dream came roaring back into his mind, and with it came the realization that it was not a dream. And that was not semantics. Jackson did not tell himself it was a nightmare instead of a dream. No, it was all too clear. Nothing in it felt like the fleeting images of a dream. These were all memories, freshly imprinted on his mind. There was a great chance that Jackson had killed again. This time, he recalled with a tremor, it had been a boy. He had shot a boy.

The former soldier had killed before. The truth was he had killed many men, but that was the point. They were men. The boy had pointed the gun and pulled the trigger, but that rationalization did nothing to assuage his anguish. The wrenching pain tearing at his emotions began to mix with the searing pain of his wounds, which he could no longer subconsciously block. They were not debilitating, but when he tried to move, it quickly dawned on him that it would be easier to stay motionless. His body would not cooperate. A quick hack started at the top of his lungs. Then three short coughs lifted his head off the pillow it was resting on. Finally, it settled into his chest and became a series of convulsions and barks. Just as quickly as it began, Jackson stopped. His mind and body fell right back into position, staring at the ceiling and pondering the events that had happened in the early morning hours. Moray and Apallion appeared to him again. The locals were pictured as well. He focused again on the boy, and it was terrible in all possible ways, but those images could not keep his mind from progressing to the horror of its eventual destination.

"Annabel!" He sat straight up in bed, shaking and sucking for air. The world was a blur as he swiftly turned his head back and forth, looking around his own bedroom, seeing it as a familiar setting, but one that seemed to belong to long ago memories. How had he gotten here? The last thing he could remember was the cameo in his hand. Everything from that moment to now was a blank. Jackson felt dizzy sitting up. There was still a low ringing in his ears. His one ear was swollen and burned with pain, as did some of his other wounds. Nausea was starting to well up in his guts, and he began to sweat. Still, he wanted to turn over and get out of bed but immediately got a quick reminder that other events must have occurred after seeing his grandmother's necklace. In simply placing his hand on his bed's mattress, which was fairly soft, he felt the pain of the previous night explode back into his body. The broken hand made him shudder and fall back onto the mattress. Once more he stared up at the ceiling, yet he no longer cared about the leak. He heard the shuffle of feet and the sweep of a dress across the floor. Jackson turned his gaze in the direction of the sound without lifting his head from the pillow that he now noticed was wet with perspiration. In the few moments before the shuffling feet arrived at the bedroom's door, he took notice of other stimuli. By the throbbing pain coming to life in his feet, he realized that he had several broken toes on both of them. There was a constant burning sensation in his hands, which forced him to bring both of them up to his face as he turned toward the ceiling again. Both hands were red and blistered. In the next moment, the arrival of the unknown made him drop his head to the side again.

She walked through the door. Jackson looked at her sideways, and said, "Lenore?" even though he could tell something was not quite right.

"Oh no, Mr. Lee. I haven't looked as good as Lenore in a long time. Our bodies are temples to the Holy Spirit, mind you, but my temple needs some repairs done." The woman laughed with genuine joy in her self-deprecation. "Now I know you must be worried about Lenore and little Ellie, but they are going to be just fine." The good tidings that she bore finally broke Jackson out of his stupefaction.

"Mrs. Clemner," was how Jackson addressed the woman as she pulled a small chair with wicker cane weaving on the back and seat over to his bedside. "What are you doing here? What's going on, Mrs. Clemner?" He suddenly felt a terrible tightness in his chest and his throat itched. As quickly as he could he turned away and began to cough. It almost reached the point of being violent, but as soon as it subsided, Jackson turned back to her. She was ready, but not with answers.

"Dr. Horner..."

"Huber!"

"No. No, Mr. Lee. Dr. Horner. Robert Horner, a young physician, not old Dr. Huber."

"Horner, Horner, right." Jackson settled back into the pillow again.

"Dr. Horner said that..."

"Mrs. Clemner, I am sorry, but can you tell me where Lenore is?" She was not offended that he interrupted. Her husband did that often. It was a look of concern with a hint of sadness that stared back at him, not anger.

"Of course, Jackson...my dear boy." She paused for a breath. "After the...the events of this morning, Lenore went to the Weikerts for help. They sent one of their boys into town to get us. By the time we got here, Lenore and Mr. Weikert had gotten things pretty stable. So, William took Lenore and Ellie back into

Gettysburg. We thought you should be taken to your house with you and Lenore not being…well you know, not being…"

"I understand," he whispered.

"So, we got you up here. Lenore wanted to stay, but I insisted that I would take care of you. She should take care of Ellie. You've been sleeping, or I guess the doctor said you were 'unconscious,' for about six hours."

"Lenore and Ellie are safe then?" Jackson was having some trouble catching his breath.

"Yes, Jackson. William has them in town. Whoever your former friends were, they won't be bold as to try something in town."

"They weren't my friends." Jackson immediately thought of Archie Galloway, but just as fast decided it would be futile, and at the moment exhausting, to try to differentiate between Archie, Moray, and Apallion.

"I'm sorry. I meant your former secessionist comrades. They were former soldiers from the South, correct?"

"Not all of them. Some were locals."

"Yes. Well, Deputy Klunk is at Lenore's farm right now, looking into the matter?"

"Are you serious? An armed mob attacks a widow and her daughter's farm and Sheriff Streeter can't be bothered to get out of his office. He only lives a few…"

"Oh my dear boy, you don't know about our good sheriff, do you?" Jackson was blinking his eyes, trying to focus on not throwing up.

"Mrs. Clemner, I'm not sure I know anything at this point." He closed his eyes because the room was starting to spin.

"Jackson, you just rest. We'll talk later. But, first, the doctor told me to give you...

"Tell me about Streeter." Even in his wounded state, Jackson knew that he had been rude. "I'm sorry, Mrs. Clemner. I'll be all right. Could you, please, tell me about the sheriff?"

"Well, from what Lenore told us, it was Sheriff Streeter that interrupted your little party." Jackson wanted to correct her on the use of the word, party, but thought better of it. Before he could speak, he realized that she was just trying to be cheerful. She was probably trying to put up a good show for him. He let her continue. "The sheriff killed one of them." Jackson prayed that it had been Moray or Apallion.

"What was his name, the man Streeter killed?"

She answered with a hint of frustration. "I'm sorry, Jackson. I don't know that."

"I see. It's all right. It's all...yeah."

"Most of them all scattered."

"Figured that would happen." Jackson's mind went back to his initial assessment of the men. Being correct gave him little comfort.

"Tragically, Sheriff Streeter was shot by one of them as they ran."

"What?" Jackson's eyes finally opened all the way.

"The doctor thinks he will live, but he is seriously wounded. That's why the doctor is not here. He had to go with the sheriff. He said he would come back as soon as he could. He told me to give you this..." Jackson started breathing a little harder but was able to stop it before he began hyperventilating.

He took two deep breaths, paused, and then asked Lenore's mother, "Mrs. Clem... Clemner. I need to know...to know something."

"Yes, Dear. What is it?"

"My wife...my wife, Annabel." It had taken a great effort to say her name. Jackson paused to catch his breath, unsure if it was her memory or his injuries that caused his distress. "Those bastards brought her casket...and her, her body. They put me...I guess...I don't know what they wanted. To break me, I guess. To break me."

"Rest now, Jackson. You take it easy. Lenore was not certain, but she thought the corp...the body might have been your wife. I'm not sure how she knew that, but she did. Lenore and Mr. Weikert returned her body to the coffin and sealed it again. They placed it in the root cellar, where it's cool, till you can tell us what you want to do."

Jackson whispered, "Thank you." Lenore's mother was upset by the talk of bodies and death. It was not that death scared her, or that she could not handle it. She had experienced a number of deaths in her family, most recently Mahlon's, of whom she had grown very fond. No, for her, it was a matter of being indelicate. It pained her to not know how to comfort someone. For several minutes she sat in silence. Jackson kept his eyes closed and simply focused on breathing. His lungs seemed clogged, as though he had a chest cold.

Suddenly, Jackson opened his eyes and asked, "Was there a boy found, a boy that had been shot?" Mrs. Clemner's eyes widened a bit.

"I don't...no, Jackson...no. Only the one rebel soldier was there when William and I got there. And he looked about your age. Terrible sight, just lying on the ground, staring up at the sky. What boy are you talking about?"

Jackson's mind was obsessing on the boy. He never made the connection to his friend, Archie, the Confederate soldier that would be about his age. After turning his head toward the ceiling so he would not have to look at her, Jackson said, "The one I shot." He heard her gasp and knew he had made a mistake telling the woman he hoped would be his future mother-in-law that he had gunned down a child.

"Oh my! Oh, I don't...Are you certain, Jackson?" Though he had just decided that it had been a mistake to tell her about this, Jackson did not like her questioning whether he would remember shooting someone. Yet, the truth was that he was tormenting himself. His next sentence would have been shocking to most anyone, but especially a member of the Society of Friends.

"Shot him right in the chest. Shot him dead. He shouldn't have been there. Why'd he have to go and point his...point that..." Jackson began to cough. The motion hurt his head terribly and he grew silent. Mrs. Clemner was becoming nervous. Lenore meant the world to her, but it had been very difficult for her and her husband to accept the fact that she had allowed this man, Jackson Lee, to court her. Her daughter said he was a good and kind man. She said that Ellie needed a father and that Jackson was taking on more of that role every day. Still, despite Jackson's efforts to ingratiate himself with Mr. and Mrs. Clemner, Lenore's mother would not fully accept him. Jackson could see all of this in her eyes, long before this bloody day of violence. The saddest truth was that she could never accept him, no matter how well he treated her daughter and granddaughter. He was a former soldier, a man of violence and death. Furthermore, he was a Southerner. Not only had he picked up a weapon and gone to war, which was anathema to a Quaker, but he had also committed treason. She had tried, over and over, to be nice to Jackson, but he knew that in Mrs. Clemner's mind, he was no Mahlon and never would be. Now, to seal that in blood, he had confessed to killing a boy.

Maria Clemner wanted nothing more than to throw a saddle on one of Lenore's horses and ride for Gettysburg. However, she had promised her daughter that she would take care of him. She swallowed hard and pushed her horror into a strong compartment within her mind. Impassively she said, "I don't know what to tell you, Mr. Lee. No one else was found at Lenore's farm." She emphasized the last two words and Jackson knew why. He was too tired, too sick, and too hurt to fight about it. He remained silent. "Now, as I was trying to say earlier, the doctor asked me to give you this." She reached for something on a nightstand, one that had been left behind by the Hess family.

"What is it?" he asked without looking.

"It's a mixture of Old Overholt whiskey and opium. Dr. Horner said it would dull the pain from all of your wounds and allow you to rest comfortably." Jackson knew what he had to do and silently got up on one elbow. Without any hesitation, he followed orders. He drank the mixture down, and then coughed several times; one for the whiskey, the rest for the smoke inhalation.

"Now you rest here, Mr. Lee. I am going to see to Deputy Klunk. See if there is anything he requires before leaving. I would think he would like to speak to you. I'll bring him up here if that's all right with you."

"It's fine, Mrs. Clemner." He brought his hand up instinctively to rub his forehead and temples, which were pounding. Right before he touched his hand to his head, the pain reminded him that his hands were burned. Touching anything would increase that sensation. Instead, he rolled his head around a little on the pillow, but this too brought renewed agony. The right side of his head, at the base of the skull, felt strange, as if something was not solid anymore. Fluid seemed to be slowly building up. He remembered being struck by something, but the memory was very fuzzy.

He could not make sense of it and turned to Lenore's mother to finish his thought, "Although I cannot promise you I will be awake when you do."

"I won't disturb you then. You just rest, Jackson. Your farm will be fine. Your friends are all gone. Most importantly, Lenore and Ellie are safe now." Despite her misgivings, or even antipathy, Mrs. Clemner wanted to put Jackson at ease. Seeing him in his present condition, she thought, would elicit sympathy from even the devil. She reached out to pat Jackson on the head but misread his turning away in pain as him turning away from her comfort. Dismissively, she quickly got up, and said, "I will be back as soon as I can." Then she walked out of the room and left the house, not bothering to even put the cork back in the bottle of Old Overholt or the cap back on the tincture of opium.

Jackson had heard her words. It was a tremendous load off of his mind to know that Lenore and Ellie were safe. However, Mrs. Clemner's statement that his farm would be fine did not sit well with him. He was injured. That was for sure. Everything from a cracked head to shotgun wounds to burned hands was afflicting him. His crops had been harvested, but the livestock would not take care of themselves. Jackson brought his head up slightly. The pain instantly made him feel an intense nausea. Perhaps the animals could get by one day without him. Maybe the Weikerts could milk the cows. Rest, to be sure, would help his head. The broken toes and fingers could be splinted. Hopefully, the burns and wounds would not grow fevered. One day of respite would not destroy his world.

With that decision made, his mind brightened ever so slightly. Now he wanted to try to make sense of what had happened. What did he remember? What had he missed? If the deputy wanted to ask him questions, he should try to be ready with some answers. He decided to go back to the beginning. What had started it all? Jackson remembered going to comfort Ellie. That had made him begin thinking about marrying Lenore once more. Before Jackson could move on to the actual proposal and the disturbing conversation about their dead spouses, Jackson refocused on Ellie. What had she told him last night? It was odd. "'The firewood will not save you. Only the door will save you."

"No. No. That wasn't it," Jackson proclaimed to no one in particular.

'The firewood and the powder will save you, but the door will not." He heard Ellie's voice saying it, but it still did not seem right.

"No. It was the reverse." The little girl's voice did not come to him this time, so he spoke the words aloud. "The firewood and the powder will not save you, but the door will." He pondered those words for a moment and then decided it was, "Will not save them. Will not save them. But the door will save you." Nothing moved or made a sound. "But who the hell is them?" The whiskey and opium were already starting to take effect. Jackson felt a beautiful, soothing warmth begin to take over his body, starting in his belly.

Just as he was beginning to slip into the feelings of euphoria, dissonance raised its ugly and unnerving head. A man's voice came from the kitchen. A mournful song echoed in Jackson's ears and mind. The opium confused him more by slowing it down. The song sounded angry, almost vengeful, but with a hint of sadness. Jackson struggled to hear the words clearly. The man was saying something about having control of God's judgment and taking revenge on his woman. The voice sounded scratchy and distant, as if coming from a megaphone used on ships. That single thought stole Jackson's attention away. Megaphones? He had no idea why he had thought of that, for he had no experience with ships. Forcing himself to focus, he looked back to the bedroom door. Jackson could make no sense of it and grew desperate to know if the voice was even real.

"Who's there?" Jackson called out. No one answered. Could it be the deputy, so soon after Mrs. Clemner's departure? The relief from his pain became more acute, and it suddenly dawned on him that he no longer cared who was there. Yet, someone was, and before Jackson could even begin to react, that someone was beside his bed.

"Miss Maria wanted me to give you a drink of water." Jackson let his head roll over to the side. It had been a day for strange appearances, and this one fit right in. Holding a cup of water was a Black man in a strangely cut suit, a style Jackson had never seen before.

"Do you work for the Clemners?" he asked before his mouth formed a strange frown.

"Why is that, Mr. Lee? A Negro tries to help you and you immediately think he's a slave or somethin'." Most people would be taken aback by the aggressive attitude of the man and would, without thinking, begin to apologize. That was not the disposition of Jackson Lee. He had never owned any slaves. None of his family or friends had. However, he would not allow some Negro to talk to him that way. This man should know his place. It raised Jackson's anger, but the medicine he had taken made him speak in a friendly voice. His rebuke came as a playful interrogation, but it was intended to make the man see his mistake.

"No. No. We got no slaves here. Ain't you heard? Mr. Lincoln set y'all free. Nah, it just seems that you Darkies are one of two things here in Adams County. Either you're a hired hand or you're a servant. I thought you might be that Sam Stanton that Mrs. Clemner was talking 'bout hiring." That was too much talking for Jackson. His body seemed to rise and go limp as he gasped for air.

"My name ain't Stanton, Mr. Lee." Jackson stared at him for a long time. Then a wave of giddiness from the medicine began to grow within him.

"Then are you that mulatto janitor, Hopkins?" asked Jackson with feigned confusion.

"No sir, I am not." Jackson felt he had turned the tables somewhat. The aggression was gone from the man's voice, replaced with his own confusion. The former southerner thought he would push it a little more.

"Well, there are few a y'all that have businesses. I know now. You're Mr. Robinson, the confectioner. Did my sweetheart, Lenore, send you..." Jackson began to cough and giggle at the same time. He shook it off and finished. With a sandpapered voice he asked, "Did she send a treat?"

"Don't have any sweets on me! No, sir!" The man's nostrils flared a little and Jackson could see the fire in his eyes. Jackson knew he had forced the man to lose his focus. Playing the game, he answered the man's anger with a sad expression.

"Right. Right. I just...I just saw Mr. Robinson a few days ago. Sorry. Must be this...this pain...this headache...Who are you again? Wait. I know. Of course. You're Solomon, the barber on Washington Street in Gettysburg. Did Mrs. Clemner send you to give me a shave and a haircut?" Jackson smiled weakly at the man. "I'm 'fraid...I'm not up for that. Sorry." A look of rage came over the man. He moved closer to Jackson.

"My name is Johnson! I am a musician. See here." The man lifted a case up and Jackson let his face fall into the mattress to look a little lower at what appeared to be a piece of luggage for carrying a guitar. He recalled a fuzzy memory of one of his comrades, sitting in front of a fire, while they were in winter camp, singing songs to entertain, but also to kill time.

"You're going to sing me a song?" The look on the man's face was growing more and more dyspeptic. Suddenly Jackson's addled brain had a flash of focused recall. He remembered a specific song that his comrade would often sing. "Can you play 'Cotton-Eyed Joe' on that thing?"

Johnson's eyes flashed with anger. He growled out, "No, sir. I don't care for the words to that song."

Jackson's voice was filled with the same wrath. "Neither do I." They stared at each other. Johnson had a fire in his eyes. Jackson's eyes were growing glassy, but within his irises, a blue blaze remained. "Who do you think you are?"

"Now you see here," the guitar player snarled. Yet, in an instant, his face became emotionless. Still, he shook his head as though he had to shake off any remaining fury. Then he looked at Jackson with a friendly expression. He tilted his head, smiled, and said, "Jack, you seem to be looking stronger, a lot stronger than some of the other times we've run into each other."

Jackson's expression did not change. The lightness in his voice, which had come from the medicine that had been administered, was now completely gone. "I think you better call me, Mr. Lee. You understand me, boy?"

"Yes, sir, Mr. Lee. Much stronger. We'll have to do something 'bout that." He finally managed to get Jackson to take the cup of water from his hand by simply releasing it. The prone man held it on his chest. The stranger knelt down and placed his case on the rough-hewn floor. He stood up, holding an acoustic guitar by the neck.

The opium and alcohol blurred Jackson's vision and made his mind feel fuzzy. "I know who you are.

You're the man with the guitar. You've come to kill me, just like before. Miss Electa and Lenore; I'll never again see my...my..." Jackson shook his head, trying to make it clear. All he could muster was, "I know you."

"Yes, sir, Mr. Lee. You do indeed know me." With that, he turned the guitar flat. He carefully brought it back, as if measuring the radius of the turn. No warning was given, as the guitar rocketed across Jackson's chest. The cup of water flew against the far wall. The violence Jackson had experienced in the early morning did not surprise him. As soon as he saw Moray and Apallion, it was expected. This was not. It shocked him. Unlike the earlier incident, he did not make a move to defend himself. "And with that fractured skull of yours, this shouldn't take long at all." The guitar was turned on edge and swiftly came crashing down on Jackson's forehead. He barely held onto consciousness, but the intense, stunning pain of the blow kept him from moving. The second blow brought complete darkness. The Black man hit him three more times for good measure. Jackson was motionless, but he could see that the young Negro was not. He was breathing heavy, more from his rage than any exertion. "How do you like that tune, Southern Man? Wrote that one just for you." He was not expecting an answer or a question.

"Why?" barely escaped from Jackson's lips.

The young man threw down what remained of his guitar and placed his hands on his hips for a moment. He was frustrated, moving into exasperation. It only took two steps to be at the head of the bed. Jackson futilely raised a hand in the direction of the sound of his steps. The stranger, with an astonishing speed, removed the pillow from under Jackson's head. The old veteran of the Army of Northern Virginia now felt the weight of his past crushing down on him. He could not make sense of anything, but he felt his life slipping away. Once more, there was no oxygen to be had, but it was a Negro's strong hands causing the asphyxiation instead of a fire. Jackson knew no one was coming to save him this time. Eight years earlier, he had left home to fight for his brothers. No other reason was necessary. Yet, here at the end, he realized he had been fighting for the status quo and that meant keeping the Negro in his place. And by God, the Negro now had his revenge. That was Jackson's last thought, and then he was gone.

Johnson followed him into the void.

The story of Jack and Hannah, Darkness at the Edge of Time, will continue in...

THE SNAKES OF STRAWBERRY HILL